The History of a Slave

H. H. Johnston

The History of a Slave

by

H. H. JOHNSTON

Edited and Introduced by

PAUL E. LOVEJOY

 Markus Wiener Publishers
Princeton

For information, write to: Markus Wiener Publishers
231 Nassau Street, Princeton, NJ 08542
www.markuswiener.com

Library of Congress Cataloging-in-Publication Data

Johnston, Harry Hamilton, Sir, 1858-1927.
    The history of a slave / by H. H. Johnston ; edited and introduced by
Paul E. Lovejoy.
      p. cm.
    First published: London : Kegan Paul, Trench, & Co., 1889.
    Includes bibliographical references.
    ISBN 978-1-55876-553-5 (hardcover : alk. paper)
    ISBN 978-1-55876-554-2 (pbk. : alk. paper)
    1. Slaves—Africa—Fiction. 2. Slavery—Africa—Fiction. 3. Africa—Social
life and customs—Fiction. 4. Indigenous peoples—Africa—Fiction.
I. Lovejoy, Paul E. II. Title.
    PR4826.J58H57 2012
    823.8—dc23
                                    2011040794

Markus Wiener Publishers books are printed in the United States of America on acid-free paper and meet the guidelines for permanence and durability of the Committee on Production Guidelines for Book Longevity of the Council on Library Resources.

Dedicated to Mark B. Duffill

Contents

Acknowledgments

I would like to thank Rachel Neufeld, who transcribed the text, checked details, and compared the book and serial versions. Abubakar Babajo Sani assisted with Hausa language details and geography. Yacine Daddi Addoun and Ismael Musah Montana assisted in identifying the "Mosque of the Olive Tree" and clarifying the issue of Johnston's confusion. In my study of trade in Adamawa, I have collaborated with Mark Duffill for several decades. His friendship and support are the reasons this book is dedicated to him.

This project has been supported by the Canada Research Chair in African Diaspora History and the Social Sciences and Humanities Research Council of Canada.

Introduction

H. H. Johnston's
The History of a Slave
and the "Scramble" for Africa

PAUL E. LOVEJOY

In 1889, British colonial official Sir Harry Johnston published *The History of a Slave*, a biographical account of a slave named Horejandu. It was originally published as a four-part serial in *The Graphic* of London on March 30, April 6, April 13, and April 20, 1889. The publishing firm Kegan Paul, Trench, & Co. published the book in the same year. Both versions included forty-eight illustrations based on Johnston's own drawings in Africa. The Kegan Paul, Trench edition also contains a short preface by Johnston that is not included in *The Graphic*. There are only minor differences between the two texts, and they do not affect meaning. This reprinted edition is based on the book and is published with annotations that explain the context and the significance of *The History of a Slave*.

Although other imperialists were more prominent, Johnston was one of the "men on the spot" who aggressively pursued British colonial expansion during the period of the "Scramble" for Africa after the Berlin Conference of 1884. Johnston's career took him to the Bight of Biafra, the Congo, the Zambezi, Lake

Nyasa, Kenya, and Uganda during the course of the Scramble. While perhaps not always the key British agent in colonial expansion, he was ubiquitous. Detailed correspondence, diaries, official reports, and other surviving papers allow for a considered idea of what Johnston knew and thought. He chronicled his exploits in an autobiography and some forty works, including several novels that he finished after he retired. In 1929, his brother published a selection of his papers in *Life and Letters of Sir Harry Johnston*. As a collector, Johnston made substantial donations to the British Museum and Kew Botanical Gardens. Some of his drawings and sketches hang in the Royal Geographical Society, and others were sold privately or remained in the family. He was aggressively opportunistic, which accounts for the convergence of his scientific curiosity and artistic ambitions with a political career.

In *The History of a Slave*, Johnston follows one man, Horejandu, from his enslavement in the grasslands of Cameroon through the commercial centers of the Central Sudan to the Mosque of the Olive Tree in Tunis. Johnston based his story on what he learned in North Africa and in the Bight of Biafra, and as he states in his introduction, he attempted to "give a realistic sketch of life in the Western Sudan" drawn from "the accounts given to me by negro slaves in the Barbary States and in Western Equatorial Africa." Although the story is revealing in its depiction of life in Africa and in its geographical descriptions, Johnston never went to the places mentioned, except Tunis. Rather, the account is most interesting because of Johnston's attitudes towards Islam, slavery, and African customs, which reflected the ideological framework of British imperial expansion during the "Scramble." Johnston used images of the spectacular and the grotesque in a shocking display of the pseudoscientific racism that pervaded British society at the end of the nineteenth century. *The History of a Slave* provides insight into the imperialist view of slavery in Africa and efforts to combat slavery as well as to end perceived barbaric practices, which became important justifications for colonial occupation.[1]

Sir Harry Johnston was born in London in 1858, the son of a wealthy insurance executive who was a member of the Royal Geographical Society and belonged to the Catholic Apostolic Church. His upbringing was therefore cosmopolitan but unusual because of religious affiliation. Best known for his involvement in British imperial expansion in Africa, Johnston wrote, among his forty books, *The River Congo* (London, 1884) and *The Kilimanjaro Expedition* (London, 1886). He was a reporter and illustrator for various British newspapers, including the *The Globe* and *The Graphic*. A series of letters on "the Tunisian Question" relating to French occupation were published in *The Globe* from January through June 1880 but were never published as a book. Johnston was also a reasonably accomplished artist, as reflected in the illustrations for *The History of a Slave*. Indeed he aspired to be a great artist and was disappointed that his major painting of the al-Zantuna mosque in Tunis was not well received in 1880. Such failure helped push him towards colonial service.

As a government employee in the Foreign Office, he took it upon himself to develop various specializations, as well as continue his painting. He was one of the first specialists in the Bantu languages, despite many errors resulting from a lack of linguistic training. Johnston was also a noted collector of botanical and zoological specimens, which were donated to the British Museum and Kew Gardens; his many contributions afforded him a veneer of scientific commitment that made his racist and fanciful accounts of Africa all the more dangerous. Nevertheless, as his biographer, Roland Oliver, has observed, Johnston's most lasting venture concerned his bold moves to advance British imperial interests.

Johnston wrote *The History of a Slave* in 1888, at the age of thirty, while he was serving in the Bight of Biafra. The Consulate in the Bights of Benin and Biafra had been established in 1849, and by the 1880s it had become the bridgehead for British expansion. Johnston was initially appointed Vice-Consul of the Oil Rivers District and Cameroon and was stationed off the Cameroon coast on the remote island of Mondoleh in Ambas Bay, across from Victoria. Johnston did very little work as Vice-Consul. Mondoleh was far from the main ports in the Bight of Biafra and the Bight of Benin and had almost no commercial importance. Instead, Johnston constructed the consulate house, which was imported from Britain and had three rooms—one painted pink, one green, and one blue. When he traveled locally, he took with him considerable baggage, including notebooks, paints, brushes, and canvas; cages for specimens; containers for botanical samples; his tame monkey, pet birds, and Muscovy ducks; and a full supporting staff of servants, transported in a large canoe paddled by his "Kru-boys" and sailors from Old Calabar.[2] According to the provisions of the Berlin Conference, however, Mondoleh and the Baptist Mission at Victoria fell into the German sphere, and Johnston had to abandon his island paradise just as Consul Edward Hewitt returned to Britain on sick leave and Johnston assumed the position of Acting Consul at Old Calabar.

Although Johnston's term as Vice-Consul was largely a sinecure, he became Acting Consul at a critical time—when British trade in the Bight of Biafra faced a crisis. There was fierce competition for control of the lucrative palm oil trade, and the Consulate played an active role in promoting British interests. British firms, mostly from Liverpool, were encouraged to consolidate to undermine the commercial control of the trade by local merchants. Johnston boldly saw an opportunity to intervene at Opobo, the principal shipping point for palm oil in the Niger delta, and thereby make a name for himself in imperial circles.[3] Even more than Consul Hewitt, Johnston promoted a cartel of Liverpool firms in a manner that undoubtedly overstepped his legal and diplomatic responsibilities as Acting Consul. Under the terms of the Berlin Conference of 1884, Britain was bound to promote free trade for all countries and merchants, including indigenous traders on the coast. Johnston's actions could have proven embarrassing for the British Government in the face of international rivalries with Germany and France. Furthermore, the Glasgow firm Miller Brothers remained outside the cartel and therefore threatened to undermine the Liverpool merchants and Johnston's ambitions. To sidestep this lack of solidarity among British merchants, Johnston forced a crisis that led to British intervention, in violation of the terms of the Berlin Conference and certainly against the wishes of local officials and merchants in the Niger delta and the interior.

To consolidate the position of the Liverpool cartel, in September 1887 Johnston kidnapped King Jaja of Opobo, the most important coastal merchant and the strongest political leader in the Bight of Biafra. Jaja was by origin a slave at Bonny before amassing considerable wealth and power and establishing his own merchant state at Opobo, in the eastern Niger delta, and becoming the major supplier of palm oil and kernels to various British firms, including Miller Brothers of Glasgow. He was well educated, and two of his sons were at school in England at the time of Johnston's intervention at Opobo. Education in England was common among merchants in the Bight of Biafra and helps to explain why merchants there could serve as middlemen in the trade in palm oil and palm kernels from the interior and in the distribution of imported goods from England and elsewhere.

Jaja and his followers had settled at Opobo a decade earlier and had built the most successful merchant organization in the palm oil trade. Johnston deceived Jaja into coming on board a naval vessel stationed at Opobo, then summarily arrested him, threatened to bombard Opobo and destroy the town, and transported Jaja to Accra to stand trial on trumped up charges. Johnston's hostility to Jaja can be explained only by Johnston's ambitions to leave his mark on British expansion. As the treatment of Jaja demonstrates, Johnston was an active and ambitious participant in British imperial expansion in the Bight of Biafra and subsequently in other parts of Africa. Moreover, Johnston detained Jaja's sons, who rushed from England to their father's side in Accra. Jaja was sentenced to exile in the Caribbean. Johnston's high-handed actions stand out not only for their illegality but also for his use of terror. Jaja's arbitrary removal in September 1887 laid the basis for the establishment of the Protectorate of the Niger, with appointed administrative councils for towns within the annexed jurisdiction. For these bold moves, Johnston had no official approval and disobeyed specific orders of restraint, which he conveniently ignored. Although the Foreign Office was greatly annoyed with Johnston's intervention, Lord Salisbury at the Foreign Office consciously chose to cover up the incident rather than discipline Johnston. Relations with Germany and France were delicate, and rather than reveal embarrassing behavior, Salisbury and the Foreign Office staff manufactured a white paper that was backdated to give the impression that intervention at Opobo was unavoidable and therefore sanctioned. Thus, the document which was prepared on April 6, 1888, was backdated to November 25, 1887, one week before Jaja's trial in Accra and well after Jaja's removal the previous September.[4] For his part, Jaja's decision to surrender to Johnston and accept exile was partly influenced by concern for the safety of his sons as well as the lives of the people in Opobo who were at risk from Johnston's threat of destroying the town without warning.

When Johnston returned to Britain in 1888 after these events and while he was finishing *The History of a Slave*, he found that he was popular in the social circles of London. At afternoon tea and over dinner, he told many fanciful stories about his exploits and experiences. Johnston was particularly scandalous in his efforts to shock effete social gatherings by describing cannibalism on the Cross River, as if he could overcome his short, boyish appearance with titillating barbarism. Such behavior is consistent with the exaggerated descriptions of violence and gruesome accounts of cannibalism and cruel executions that feature in *The History of a Slave*. These details are more revealing about Johnston and the circle in which he moved than about his subjects in Africa.

As is clear in his descriptions of various places in the Sokoto Caliphate, where he had never been, Johnston was familiar with the geography and to some extent the political landscape of the Central Sudan. In *The History of a Slave*, Johnston's invention of cannibalism on the Cameroon grassfields helped him construct a credible story of a "pagan" slave that drew on his research into matters of ethnicity, trade routes, and the political context of the Muslim Central Sudan and Sahara. Oliver describes Johnston's *History of a Slave* as a picaresque novel, but this insight appears to overlook or reject circumstantial evidence that the text is biographical in nature and not at all improbable, except for the exaggerations of barbarity. Johnston could not have known the details recounted in the text unless there were personalized dimensions he had gleaned through his experience in Tunis and subsequently on the Cross River. We cannot know if Johnston relied on one or several sources, but the hidden hand of the informants is evident. This is revealed especially in Johnston's use of the Hausa language. In virtually all cases where he employs Hausa words, his usage is correct. It is unlikely that he had access to Hausa informants anywhere other than in Tunis, and hence the details and idea of a "story" must have dated to his residence there in the winter and spring of 1879-1880, when he went there for health reasons and to paint and sketch.[5]

The History of a Slave recounts the adventures of an individual slave, shaped by Johnston's drawing on his experiences in Tunis and the Bight of Biafra and merging them with his extensive reading of the existing geographical accounts of the Central Sudan. Horejandu, which Johnston says means "big head" in Fulfulde, was born in the Cameroon grassfields. Johnston gives the name of Horejandu's mother as Tutu, a junior wife of Asho-eso, the "elephant killer," whose senior wife, Ndeba, figures prominently because of her execution as a suspected witch. The description of her trial by ordeal, the masquerade, the importance of Ñgañga, the Epfumo house, and the *Ndoge* brotherhood are reasonable depictions of the Ekpe society that prevailed in the Cross River region and its interior. As a child, Horejandu had the name Mvu, which Johnston says means "dog," but after Horejandu's puberty rituals, he was renamed Mitwo, which Johnston says means "big head" in Horejandu's native language, Mbudikum (a term that applied to peoples who occupied the grasslands north of Mt. Cameroon and at the time were organized into about 150 small chieftaincies).[6] His Muslim slave name was Horejandu, which Johnston states also means "big head" in Fulfulde. It is instructive that his mother's lover has the name Ngwi, which supposedly means leopard in Mbudikum. The Ekpe society was a leopard society, and the masquerade was a leopard. The discussion of cannibalism, funeral rituals, and trial by ordeal should be seen in this context. In *The History of a Slave*, Johnston had no reason to be scientific about his descriptions, but he was a collector, a classifier, and an artist, and the anthropological dimensions are consistent with this amateur fascination. The places in *The His-*

tory of a Slave are real, and the events in the account are realistic, other than the exaggerated barbarity that reflects the imperial mindset.

The itinerary of Johnston's Mbudikum pagan—going north into the Sokoto Caliphate, across the Sahara, and to Tunis—can be mapped with considerable historical accuracy. Although many slaves from the grasslands went to the coast at Duala, Bimbia, and Old Calabar, and some were even sent on slave ships to the Americas, especially to Brazil and Cuba, the grassfields were increasingly subjected to enslavement from Adamawa and the movement of slaves into the Sokoto Caliphate after the middle of the nineteenth century. Johnston pieced his notes together in realizing that someone he had met in Tunis quite possibly could have come from Adamawa and therefore might have been Mbudikum. Johnston had an imagination, as is revealed in his social behavior, his art, and his choice to live in isolation. According to the story, Horejandu is enslaved because of the aggressive push of Fulbe or Fulani warriors southward from Adamawa into the grassfields. The events were occurring at a time not only when the jihad from the Sokoto Caliphate was being pursued but also when long-distance caravan trading was being established from the north.[7] Horejandu's travels took him to several of the emirates in Adamawa, including Tibati, Banyo, Ngaundere, and Yola. He eventually lived in Bauchi and passed through Keffi and Zaria on his way to Kano, where he was a slave to an indigo dyer and worked at a marina and a dyeing center, of which there were many in and near Kano. He was given a wife, Erega, who was Tiv in origin, and who endured the suffering of the desert crossing with him.

In contrast to Oliver's interpretation that the book is a work of historical fiction, I would suggest that the book is actually a biography of a young man whom Johnston must have met in

Tunis and apparently befriended, probably near the al-Zaytuna Mosque, which Johnston refers to as the "Mosque of the Olive Tree."[8] During the eight months in 1879-1880 when he lived in Tunis, he spent considerable time painting the mosque and street scenes near the mosque. While the mosque became the focus of his study, the grand canvas that he produced was apparently not well received back in London. He displayed and sold numerous sketches and smaller paintings, and he projected his romanticism into *The History of a Slave*, but what happened to the main painting is a mystery. Moreover, the illustration of the Mosque of the Olive Tree that he published in *The Graphic* in 1889 as well as in *The History of a Slave* is not actually the al-Zaytuna Mosque but the adjacent Sulaymania Madrasa.[9] Johnston was in Tunis on the eve of French occupation, during which time he learned some Arabic. Johnston apparently came to know young men who had crossed the Sahara from the Central Sudan, and who spoke Hausa. But he was confused about the mosque, or else he did not think the public would know the difference.

Johnston saw Africa as a source of new knowledge that would benefit both his career and Britain at large. He was attracted to travel and undertook the planning of dream "camping trips," which would later be called safaris. During his idyllic years on Mondoleh, he developed the idea of *The History of a Slave*. As Johnston's later work on the Bantu languages demonstrates, he was fascinated by language. While he was in Tunis, he not only learned colloquial Arabic but also acquired some ability to understand if not speak Hausa. As is evident in *The History of a Slave*, Johnston used the Hausa that he knew to enhance the story of someone he had in his mind when he composed the book, suggesting that he embellished a biography with considerable extrapolation and insertion of fanciful details, as well as adding his own illustrations. He identifies the main character

in *The History of a Slave* as ethnically Mbudikum. Johnston
would not have met anyone in Tunis who would have been
known there as Mbudikum. In Tunis, sub-Saharan Africans
were known as "Hausa" or "Borno," indicating that they came
via either the Sokoto Caliphate, where Hausa was the common
language, or Borno, where Kanuri was the common language.
Further ethnic distinctions were not recognized in Tunis. His
preoccupation with Bantu studies apparently led to his projec-
tion of ethnic origins on those whom he presumably met in
Tunis, who would have been identified as coming from
Adamawa, where raiding, as described in *The History of a Slave*,
was common. Johnston acquired knowledge of the interior of
Cameroons while he was in the Bight of Biafra, where he met
Mbudikum "with whom I have conversed at Old Calabar."[10] Indeed, Johnston's description of Adamawa, Bauchi, and other
parts of the Sokoto Caliphate accords well with the historical
record.[11]

As Johnston states in his preface, the illustrations were not
of actual scenes that he witnessed, since Johnston did not travel
through the Sokoto Caliphate or cross the Sahara, and he did
not even reach the grasslands north of Mt. Cameroon, ascend-
ing inland only as far as the upper Cross River. And we have
seen that even what he referred to as the Mosque of the Olive
Tree was in fact the nearby Sulaymania Madrasa. The cavalier
approach that is apparent in his observations extended to his
conception of the imperial mission during the "Scramble."
Johnston was an observer and a collector, and he wrote exten-
sively in his diaries and published prolifically. His own testi-
mony indicates that he interviewed slaves from the interior of
the Cross River, in whom he took an interest because of his
study of Bantu languages, just as he collected specimens for Kew
Gardens. It is not surprising that he was able to piece together
information that enabled him to appreciate the historical sig-

nificance of the Muslim incursion from Adamawa into the Cameroon grassfields. He understood that Muslim states were consolidating their control of the Central Sudan through a continuous jihad and the enslavement of non-Muslims. This knowledge not only underlies *The History of a Slave* but also contextualizes Johnston's attitudes toward the issue of slavery at the time of British imperial expansion.

As has been articulated elsewhere, the suppression of the slave trade and attacks on slavery in Africa were used to justify the European conquest of the continent in the last two decades of the nineteenth century, precisely when *The History of a Slave* was published. Johnston documents the significance of slavery at the time. His approach to imperialism required no justification, as his manner of dealing with King Jaja demonstrates. While Johnston does not attempt in *The History of a Slave* to lay the basis of an "abolitionist" impetus for British expansion, he implicitly indicates that British imperial rule had to confront practices regarded as barbaric, such as cannibalism and trial by ordeal, as well as social issues that had already been resolved in the British Empire, such as slavery. Johnston was an active participant in the "Scramble for Africa," and as such his work is as notable for its reflection of the imperial mindset as it is for its own insights.

Thus, while *The History of a Slave* is a realistic text, identifying places and languages with a degree of accuracy that provides a snapshot of life during the late nineteenth century in the interior of the Bight of Biafra and the Central Sudan, the depiction of events and people tells us a great deal about the rhetoric of conquest and its role in justifying imperial actions that were anything but legal. Johnston reveals how he used knowledge that he acquired in Africa to advance British interests and personal gain. His text must be read with the understanding that he, like all authors—particularly "enlightened imperialists"—

had an agenda in his writing. But compared with other books in this genre, Johnston's *The History of a Slave* stands out as one of the most dramatic and lively portraits of Africa in the nineteenth century.

Sokoto Caliphate, c. 1889.

The Mosque of the Olive Tree.

Al-Zaytuna Mosque, 1880.

Notes to the Introduction

1. Paul E. Lovejoy, *Transformations in Slavery: A History of Slavery in Africa* (New York: Cambridge University Press, 3ᵈ ed., 2011), 244-63.
2. Kru mariners came from Cape Mesurado and the adjacent coast in present-day Liberia and were hired up and down the coast as sailors, working in gangs under recruiters, who were themselves Kru who had been engaged in previous contracts. See George Brooks, *The Kru Mariner in the Nineteenth Century: An Historical Compendium* (Newark, DE: Liberian Studies Association in America, 1972).
3. For the importance of the incident, see Martin Lynn, *Commerce and Economic Change in West Africa: The Palm Oil Trade in the Nineteenth Century* (Cambridge: Cambridge University Press, 1998); Robin Law, ed., *From Slave Trade to "Legitimate" Commerce: The Commercial Transition in Nineteenth-Century West Africa* (Cambridge: Cambridge University Press, 1995); and Susan Hargreaves, "The Political Economy of Nineteenth-Century Bonny: A Study of Power, Authority, Legitimacy, and Ideology in a Delta Trading Community" (Ph.D. thesis, University of Birmingham, 1987). See also Sylvanus J. S. Cookey, *King Jaja of the Niger Delta: His Life and Times, 1821-1891* (New York: Nok Publishers, 1974).
4. Roland Oliver, *Sir Harry Johnston and the Scramble for Africa* (London: Chatto & Windus, 1957), 122-23.
5. Harry H. Johnston, *The Story of My Life* (Garden City, NY: Garden City Publishing Company, 1923), 45, 51-55.
6. According to Jean-Pierre Warnier, slaves from the grassfields were known as Mburikum, Mbrikum, Mbudikum, and Mbudikom, all variations on the same term: Jean-Pierre Warnier, *Echanges, développement et hierarchies dans le Bamenda précolonial, Cameroun* (Stuttgart: Franz Steiner, 1985); and Jean-Pierre Warnier, "The Transfer of Young People's Working Ethos from the Grassfields to the Atlantic Coast," *Social Anthropology* 14, 1 (2006), 93-98. See also M. J. Rowlands, "Local and Long-Distance Trade and Incipient State Formation in the Bamenda Plateau in the Late Nineteenth Century," *Paideuma. Mitteilungen zur Kulturkunde* 25 (1979), 1-19.

7. M. B. Duffill and Paul E. Lovejoy, "Merchants, Porters, and Teamsters in the Nineteenth-Century Central Sudan," in Catherine Coquery-Vidrovitch and Paul E. Lovejoy, eds., *The Workers of African Trade* (Beverly Hills: Sage Publications, 1985), 137-67; and M. B. Duffill, ed., *The Biography of Madugu Mai Gashin Baki* (Los Angeles: Crossroads Press, 1984).

8. Johnston, *The Story of My Life*, 54. See also Oliver, *Sir Harry Johnston*, 7-17.

9. Johnston's drawing depicts arches that look exactly like the ones at the Sulaymania Madrasa, which has alternating black and white stones or bricks, whereas the Zaytuna Mosque has only one type of stone, which is red. Johnston was apparently confused because the two buildings are almost adjacent to each other. I wish to thank Yacine Daddi Addoun and Ismael Musah Montana for their discussion of Johnston's confusion.

10. H. H. Johnston, *The History of a Slave* (London: Kegan Paul, Trench, & Co., 1889), vi.

11. For slave raiding in Adamawa, see Sa'ad Abubakar, *The Lamibe of Fombina: A Political History of Adamawa, 1809-1901* (Zaria, 1979); Ahmadou Sehou, "L'esclavage dans les lamidats de l'Adamaoua (Nord-Cameroun), du début du XIXᵉ a la fin du XXᵉ siècle" (Thèse pour le Doctorat, Université de Yaounde I, 2010); and Philip Burnham, "Raiders and Traders in Adamawa: Slavery as a Regional System," *Paideuma. Mitteilungen zur Kulturkunde* 41 (1995), 153-76.

THE HISTORY
OF A SLAVE

By

H. H. Johnston, F.R.G.S., F.Z.S., &c.

Author of 'The Kilimanjaro Expedition,' Etc.

WITH 47 FULL-PAGE ILLUSTRATIONS ENGRAVED FACSIMILE
FROM THE AUTHOR'S DRAWINGS

LONDON
KEGAN PAUL, TRENCH, & CO., 1 PATERNOSTER SQUARE
1889

اب القوة

'I am not an old man yet, am I?'

PREFACE

IN accompanying this little book with prefatory remarks I fear lest I may seem to be overestimating its importance; but my publishers think a few words of explanation necessary, which will better enable readers to understand the character and the purport of what I have herein written and drawn.

The 'History of a Slave' is an attempt to give a realistic sketch of life in the Western Sudan. It is the outcome of some considerable experience of the Dark Continent, but it is especially based on what I have seen and heard when traveling in the North Africa, in the Niger Delta, and on the Cross River. I have pieced together the accounts given me by negro slaves in the Barbary States and in Western Equatorial Africa, especially by Mbudikum[1] people, with whom I have conversed at Old Calabar.

While this little work does not pretend to topographical accuracy—especially in countries that are only known to us by native reports—yet, to speak colloquially, it is not all humbug. Many of the incidents herein related I have actually witnessed during some one of my journeys in Africa. The places and peoples I have named are of real existence, as are also the languages quoted, though some of them, as in the case of the Mbudikum tongue, probably appear in print for the first time.

Were it not for the time and care which I have spent on the forty-seven illustrations of this booklet, I should consider even the few foregoing remarks superfluous; but, for the sake of these drawings, I would ask the reader to treat me somewhat seriously. These illustrations are truthful delineations of African life and scenery, and have most of them been done in Africa from actuality, though it does not necessarily follow that their application is to be exactly localised; that is to say, that, though the drawing may not have been actually done from the scene described in the book, it depicts an analogous scene elsewhere, from which, all or in part, it has been taken. It may, however, be well to mention that I have endeavoured to make my landscapes, architecture, implements, costumes—or the want of them—and studies of human types, as locally accurate as possible.

H. H. Johnston.
LONDON: *March*, 1889.

ILLUSTRATIONS

23

THE HISTORY
OF A SLAVE

CHAPTER I.

HOW do I know when I was born? We black men cannot remember the number of years that we have lived. Perhaps it was forty years ago—I don't know, I am not an old man yet, am I? You see my muscles are strong and firm, my teeth are sound, my skin is smooth and shining, and not puckered and scaly, as it is with old men. And I know that I am not young, because I have left my country in the land of the blacks for a long, long time, and when I was first caught by the slavers I was a strong full-grown man, already married. What curious people you Europeans are! You ask so many questions, and you want to know so much about things that do not concern you. Why should you care about slaves from the Sudan, and how they live, and what languages they speak? See, you have written many words already that I have spoken of, Marghi[2] and Fulde,[3] and Mbudikum and Batta,[4] and other tongues of the barbarians and pagans, who know not God, and reject the teaching of His Prophet. I too, was like them once. The country where my mother bore me is far away—far, far away, beyond the Desert, beyond the Great River, beyond the kingdoms of the Muslemin, in a land of Kufar (unbelievers), where the people, my brothers, went naked, and knew not shame. It is a country so far that, though you may love travelling, I doubt if you would ever reach it: yet once or

27

twice I have heard that white men have been near my mother-
land. They came—I have heard it said—to spy out the country
and the chiefs of the Ful people, and the Wazir of Bornu afforded them protection. Then, too, I have heard that the great
rushing river, which was distant a month's walk from my home,
towards the north—the river that the Ful-be[5] call Mayo
Fumbina,[6] and the Batta call the Benue—that this water flowed
towards the setting sun, where it joined the Kwara,[7] which
comes from Timbuktu; and up this Kwara they used to say that
white men came in big ships to buy slaves. The white men, I
heard, would come to Nufe,[8] and sometimes the Arabs have
told me they were English, and sometimes they said they were
another kind of Englishmen called Mera-kani.[9] And once, too,
some white men came up the Benue River in a steamer, and
now the Bornu people bring news to Tarabulus[10] that the white
men have got houses on the Benue, where they trade with the
Ful people. It may be lying, it may be true, I do not know; but
you white men are wonderful, and so are the things you do.

Are you going to write my history in a book? The Sidi, my
master, said you wished to do so, and as he likes you, and wishes
to please you, he has sent me here, and told me I am to do your
bidding. If you wish me to be silent, I am to be silent; if you
wish me to talk, I am to tell you all that I know, if it be words
of the Ertana[11] of the Pagans, or if it be of all the things that I
have seen and done in all my life, since I was born. Oh, yes! I
will tell you truth—by God, I will not lie—why should I? You
white men know everything, and if you found I was deceiving
you, you would send me away, and my master would punish me;
and I like coming to see you, it makes me proud to talk to a
white man—all my friends say, 'See, Abu-l-Guwah[12] must be a
man with something in him, or the Englishman would not send
for him every day, and write down in a book the words that he
speaks.'

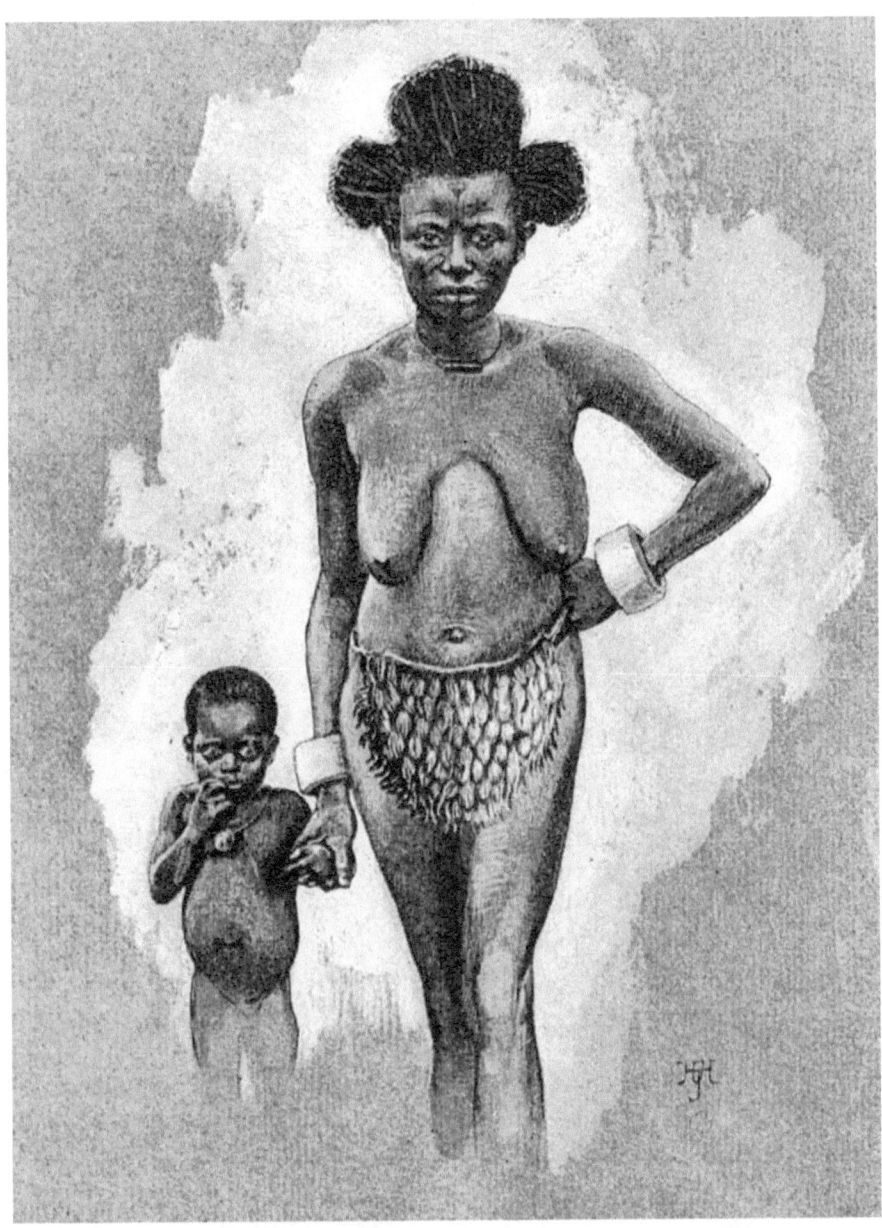

*'My mother was a young woman who had a pleasant face although,
after the fashion of these pagans, it was scarred and tattooed
on the forehead, and cheeks, and chin.'*

'We lived in a kind of compound, the four sides of which were houses built of clay, with palm-thatch roofs.'

CHAPTER II.

THE name they called my mother-country was Mbudikum. It was a land of forests and mountains—a land where water never failed, because in all directions there were brooks and rivers, and my country-people never thought of digging wells. When I can first remember, I was a small, small boy, and I lived in a large village of this country called Bahom.[13] My mother was a young woman who had a pleasant face, although, after the fashion of these pagans, it was scarred and tattooed on the forehead, and cheeks, and chin. My mother was one of the five wives of a man called Asho-eso, who was the chief of the village, and also ruled over three other neighbouring towns. We lived in a kind of compound, the four sides of which were houses built of clay, with palm-thatch roofs; in the middle of the compound or yard was a small tree growing, and on this tree were hung the skulls of people whom my father, the old chief, had killed, and there were also a lot of charms and gri-gris,[14] such as these pagans believe in, tied round the trunk of this tree; and every now and then, when the men of the village killed a slave or a prisoner whom they had captured when they fought with the Bakuba[15]—the Bakuba were a tribe who lived on a high mountain two days' journey from our village, and who used sometimes to fight with us—when, I say, the men of our town killed someone and roasted his flesh for a feast—for my people were man-eaters like the Ghuls[16] of the desert—the bones of the men they had eaten were laid round about the base of this tree.

The first thing I remember clearly was playing with the skull of one of these people whom the young men of the town had eaten. I used to roll it about on the ground of the compound, and amuse myself by filling it with sand, and then holding it up to let the sand run out from the eyes and nose. There were a number of other boys—perhaps eight or ten— living with me in the compound, who were said to be my father's children. My mother was the youngest of his wives. Her name was Tutu, and the name of the head-wife was Ndeba. I hated Ndeba, and she did not like me, because she was jealous of my mother, and her own children had died. The old chief, my father, they said had been a strong man when he was young, and they had made him chief because he had fought very bravely against the Bakuba, and had captured many prisoners and women and goats and sheep, and, as he was very generous, they made him chief in the place of another man who had been killed; but, when I remember him, he was old and his eyes were dim; he had a short grey beard, and the hair of his head was grey and he had lost many of his teeth. His knees were swollen and large, and he could only walk slowly and with a stick. For hours together he would sit on his haunches over the fire in his own hut, and do nothing but take snuff occasionally out of a small antelope-horn which hung round his neck. Only when the women wrangled too loud would he raise himself and find his voice, and when he was angry and shouted, the brightness came back to his eyes, and his voice was strong, and it made us tremble, because it was told that once in his younger days, when a wife had refused to stop yelling because the head-wife had taken her portion of peppers, he struck her on the head with his ebony stick, and she died.

Sometimes I used to creep into my father's hut and watch him as he sat over the fire; he never spoke much to me, and much of what he said seemed to be nonsense. A few sentences of his talk I still remember; he said them over and over again, like a kind of song: 'The elephants came down from the mountains—two, three elephants came. They wasted my farm, they dragged down my plantains, and they trampled my maize, and

'My father . . . was old, and his eyes were dim: he had a short grey beard,
and the hair of his head was grey, and he had lost many of his teeth. . . .
For hours together he would sit on his haunches over the fire in his own hut.'

I, Eso, I, the chief, did a cunning thing against them, for I dug a big, big pit, and I overlaid its mouth with thin sticks, and on these sticks I reared the maize stalks upright, as though they were growing, and I scattered grass about in between them, so that none might know that the sticks hid the mouth of the pit, and when the elephants came at night to eat my plantains, they pressed on the sticks, and one, the biggest, fell into the pit, and there, I, Eso, found him, and I cut the tendons of his feet so that he could not walk, and I and my men stuck him in many places with spears, so that he bled to death, and for many days we feasted on his flesh, till our bellies ached with food. And his tusks, one I sold to a Tibari[17] trader, and the other I made into bracelets for my wives, and that is why they call me "Asho-eso," the "elephant-killer."' And this tale he would tell many times, until I wearied of it, and little else he would say, except when the women quarreled, and he could not sleep.

My eldest brother was a big young man. He was the son of the second wife. I liked him because he was kind to me, and because he, too, hated the eldest wife. When she quarreled with my mother he took my mother's part. His own mother we all laughed at, because she had once broken her leg, and when it mended the bone stuck out in a lump, and one leg was shorter than the other, so that, when she walked, she walked with a hop. We called her the 'Hyena,' because her gait was limping—and in our language we call the hyena the 'limping leopard'—but my eldest brother was good to me, and would play with me, and when he took part in these pagan feasts, he would bring back a little of the man's heart they had eaten, so that I might taste it, and grow brave for Wallah! I was a pagan and a man-eater, too. I knew no better, and was as a brute, and none had told me of Allah and his Nabi.[18]

My eldest brother taught me to make bows and arrows—the bow out of the springy wood of the climbing palm, and the

string, too, of palm fibre or the twisted gut of a goat—and our
arrows were made out of stout grass-stems and notched, or
sometimes the blacksmith of the village would beat me out a
small barb of iron, which I would fasten on to the end of my
arrow. With these bows and arrows I soon learned to kill small
birds, which I took home to eat. I always shared them with my
brothers, as was our custom, for we shared everything—we
boys—but if the women tried to take something of what we had
killed to put in their own pots, we made a great noise and
stoned them, and my mother would scream and shout at the
other women if they tried to take away the things I had killed,
for my mother set much store by me, and would let no one do
me hurt if she could prevent them.

And I learned to fish in the brooks, where we made weirs of
reeds and bush-creepers, and once I remember, when I jumped
into the deep water of one of these pools, which we had
dammed up, to catch in my arms a large fish that was entrapped
there, a big lizard, such as the Arabs call 'Waran,' attacked me,
for he, too, was after the fish, and with his long, sharp-edged
tail cut the skin all down my right thigh, and I thought I should
have died, because so much blood ran out, and I could hardly
drag myself home, where my mother wailed over me; and because the head-wife was learned in medicine, and knew the best
way to stop the flowing of blood and heal the wound, my
mother had to give her a large present—I think she gave her a
goat—that she might apply her skill to close up the wound in
my thigh; and this she did, as I remember, by washing it, and
putting on it the red paste of a wood that was bitter to the taste,
and then she strapped up the whole thigh in plantain leaves,
and in a few days I was well.

CHAPTER III.

ABOUT this time a great trouble came on us, for my elder brother went out to hunt the elephant with some young men of the town. They would follow the elephants till they came to a great marsh, which was a long day's journey from the town, and here, hiding among the reeds, where the elephants came to drink and bathe, they would let fly at them with spears and poisoned arrows, hoping, by much noise and by gradually closing on them, to drive the elephants out of the clear water into the thick mud, where they would stick, and where the men could get close to them and kill them without the elephants having the power to escape or to run at the men. But one elephant, that was stronger and more cunning than the others, would not fly before the shouting, but turned round and made straight at my brother, whom he seized with his trunk and carried to the firm land among the bushes; and here, though he was like a porcupine for the lances and darts and arrows that stuck in his hide, thrown by the young men who were my brother's companions, he desisted not from his purpose, but, placing him on the ground with his trunk, he knelt down and drove one of his great tusks through my brother's body and then broke away from the young men, so that none saw in what direction he escaped through the forest, he bearing all the time my brother's body spitted on his tusk. And when the news was brought home, it was said everywhere that it was witchcraft, that some enemy of my brother's had entered into this elephant as a devil, so that he might bring about my brother's death, and I heard the women whisper that the enemy who had done this was my father's head-wife; and the poor Hyena, as we called my brother's mother, was mad for rage, and threw herself on the head-wife, biting and striking her until my father roared in his angry voice, and the other women pulled her off and tied her with bush-rope, and then for two days there was quiet; but the young men had found part of my brother's body in the forest, and had brought it back to the town, and then I heard it said that 'Epfumo' was out to find who had bewitched my brother, and entered the elephant to kill him.[19]

When I heard the great 'Bong! bong!' of the 'Etum,' which is a kind of drum made of a hollow-sounding wood, that gives out a noise almost like a bell, I was frightened and ran to my mother, she everywhere looking for me to hide me with herself in the house; for you must know the custom was, when this Epfumo was out, that he should slay all women and children, and all youths who were uninitiated, whom he met in his path. And the reason of this was, that these pagans believe that Epfumo is a 'Shaitan,' a great devil, who is able to search out the truth.

He appears like a man dressed in a great mantle made of palm-fronds, a mantle which descends from his shoulders to his knees, and is very broad and constructed somewhat like a cage, but there are holes to let the arms pass out through, and on to his finger-nails are fastened leopards' claws. In one hand he holds a great cutlass, and in the other a pierced antelope-horn, with which he blows a strong blast at times, to warn people out of his way. On his head is a hideous mask of painted wood, from the top of which hangs down behind a black-and-white monkey-skin.

When I was a child I thought that the Epfumo was a real devil, but now I know it is only a man dressed up, and generally the 'doctor,' the pagan priest of the town, and this Epfumo that came out to find the person who bewitched my brother must have been an old man named 'Asho-ntshoñ,' which means in our language 'Kill-thief.' And all this time that the Epfumo was

'But ome elephant that was stronger and more cunning than the others would not fly before the shouting, but turned round and made straight at my brother, whom he seized with his trunk and carried to the firm land among the bushes.'

searching through the town for the bewitcher of my brother, the drum in the fetish-house was going 'Bong! bong! bong!' and there was no other sound in the town but the noise of the drum, except when a dog howled or the fowls cackled; and I hid myself in the darkness of my mother's hut, fearing to let go her hand, and she, too, was frightened, and had put the screen of latticed palm-stems against the doorway of her hut; but presently we heard quite close to the entrance to our compound a blast from the Epfumo's horn.

My mother started up and trembled all over. 'He is coming in here,' she said, 'I knew it; it is the head-wife that has bewitched thy brother;' and although I was very frightened, I was very curious to see what the Epfumo would do, so I crept close to the doorway and peeped through the cracks of the palm-lattice, and for the first time I saw the terrible Epfumo. He came into the compound, walking at the head of a troop of other devils, dressed somewhat like himself, but with white staves in their hands and no cutlass, and the Epfumo cried, with a loud voice, 'I smell the witch who has bewitched Ejok' (that was my brother's name), and at these words I saw my father come out of the house, walking very slowly and painfully, and helping himself with his stick, and he said, 'What seek-est thou here, Epfumo?' and the devil said, 'I seek the bewitcher of Ejok, and I know I am near,' and the Epfumo walked towards our house, or rather he danced towards us with a curious mincing step, and again I shut my eyes with fright, for I saw he was coming to our door, and all this time my mother was crouching on the ground, putting her hands before her eyes; and when I looked out again the Epfumo had passed on, and he went very near the next house, and the next, but stopped at none till he came to the house of the head-wife, and there he danced in; and then I heard a frightful yell, and the Epfumo came out, dragging the head-wife by the wrist, and she in her scare set both her feet together and bent her body, so that he might fail to move her from the threshold of her hut; but it was of no use, for my father said, 'Bind her,' and the other dressed-up men that accompanied Epfumo took coils of bush-rope from underneath their mantle of palm-leaves, and bound the head-wife round and round, so that she was stiff, and could move nothing about her but her head; and all the while she screamed and screamed, until her screams became like the hoarse cry of an angry camel, and then when she was bound they lifted her up, and carried her out of the compound. And then after some little time the 'Bong! bong! bong!' of the fetish drum stopped, for the witch was found. And the town came to life again.

My mother rose up and lifted away the door from the entrance to her hut, made up the embers of the fire, and then rushed out into the compound to meet the other women, who were already raising a mighty clamour with their tongues. They were all shouting, 'Did I not tell you so, did I not say the head-wife had bewitched Ejok? Were not her ways always the ways of a witch? Aha, now she will be punished as she deserves!' My mother screamed the loudest of all, for she was glad, and hated the head-wife, and I shouted too and the other boys, and the small girls beat with sticks on the wooden drums, and the goats baaed and the fowls cackled, and there was a great clamour. Only my father sat quiet on his haunches and seemed sad. He said once or twice, 'Witch or no witch, she was a wise woman, and who will tend me now she is gone?' Then some young men came rushing in and said the trial would take place as soon as the moon was up.

And all that day was hard to pass. I longed so to see what they would do with the woman who had bewitched my brother; and at last the evening meal was over and it was dark, and, lighting a bundle of palm shreds at the fire, which these pagans use as torches, my mother took me by the hand and led me out

Epfumo.

of the compound, all the other women going too; but as we passed the open door of my father's hut his fire flickered up, and I saw him sitting there alone musing over the hearth, his chin resting on his hands, which held his ebony staff. And I said to my mother, 'Is he not going too?' and she said, 'He is too feeble to walk so far, and besides, he is too old to care for anything now but his soup and his snuff and she laughed. But the limping Hyena, the second wife, as she passed, said to my mother, 'It is not well to laugh, for Asho-eso was a strong man once, and it is you young women who have taken away his strength from him.'

So we passed out into the darkness, and my mother separated herself from the other wives, and here and there we saw the flare of the other torches, for many people were wending their way to the place of trial. But my mother walked not with the other wives, saying she liked not their company; and as we passed a new house that had been built in the town, a young man, a fine tall proper fellow—his name was 'Ngwi,' or 'the leopard'—came out from under the eaves of the house and looked in my mother's face as she held up her torch, and my mother nodded to him and let go my hand, holding Ngwi's in-stead, whilst she still held up her torch to light the way. Then presently she saw the other wives of my father a little way in advance, and she told me to run on ahead and go with my brothers, for there was something she must say to Ngwi first. So I ran on and joined myself to the limping Hyena, who was very sad, and sobbed and cried still, to think of the death of her son.

And when we arrived at the place of trial we found it was a large open space in the forest, where the ground was smooth and had been beaten hard by men's feet, and all vegetation was removed except for one great tree, with spreading branches, which grew in the middle of the clearing, and all round the bor-der of this maidan, or square, there were great fires burning, so that the place was full of light, and round these fires were squat-

'There were great fires burning, so that the place was full of light, and round these fires were squatting or standing all the young men of the town.'

ting or standing all the young men of the town. Most of them
were drunk with palm-wine, and kept shouting and singing
without any sense, and close to the base of the big tree there
lay my father's head-wife, still in her bonds; she could only
move her head a very little from side to side, and her eyes rolled
dreadfully; and there was another thing close beside her which
made me feel very sad and sick—it was the remains they had
found of my brother when he had been killed by the elephant,
only the head and trunk and part of his thighs were there.

Then presently there was a blowing of horns, and into the
square came Asho-ntshoñ, the old 'Ñgañga,'[20] or medicine-man
of the town, who used to dress up as the Epfumo, but this time
he was not Epfumo at all, or the women and children would
not have been there. The old Ñgañga had painted a curious
pattern of white lines over his body, and he had a lot of charms
hung about his neck, a tall plaited hat on his head, and ruffs of
white goat's fur round his ankles. He blew a loud blast on his
antelope horn, and all the noise and talking ceased; then in the
midst of silence he said, 'Epfumo has found the witch who
brought about the death of Ejok; it is Ndeba, the wife of Asho-
eso, the chief.' At these words the other wives of my father—
except my mother, who had not come—all said, 'Aya, aya! it is
true,' but the Ñgañga blew another blast on his horn to silence
them, and went on, 'Ndeba denies that she bewitched Ejok, so
it shall be put to the test, and we will see if Epfumo was wrong.'
Then, after saying these words, he took his knife and cut off a
small piece—just about a mouthful—of the flesh of my dead
brother, and called to one of his attendants, who brought a
small wooden box, in which was kept a red sauce. Into this
sauce he dipped the morsel of my brother's flesh, and rolled it
round two or three times; then he bade them hoist up Ndeba,
the head-wife, and whilst they held her upright he said to her,
'Open thy mouth and swallow this piece of the flesh of the man

whom Epfumo says thou didst bewitch. If it stays on thy stomach thou wilt be set free, and Epfumo will have told a lie, for all men will see that thou couldst not have bewitched Ejok if his substance will unite with thine; but if thou vomit up this piece of his body, Epfumo will have shown truly that thou art the witch.' Then the head-wife opened her mouth and received the morsel of my brother's flesh; and I saw the muscles of her face and throat working as though trying to swallow it, but perhaps the sauce in which it was dipped made her retch, or perhaps after all she was a witch—how do we know? perhaps there is some truth in what these pagans tell! are they not the children of Iblis? How it was I know not, but Ndeba shook all over and vomited forth the piece of flesh that had been put into her mouth.

Then a great cry went up from among the people; they all shouted 'Ndeba is the witch, Ndeba is the witch; Epfumo never tells a lie,' and the young men beat on their drums and blew their antelope-horns, and the limping Hyena, Ejok's mother, gave a sobbing scream, and rushed forward at Ndeba, who had fallen down on the ground, for the young men had left off holding her up. The Hyena tore Ndeba's face with her nails, and smashed in her nose with her fist, and would perhaps have killed her in her rage, only the Ñgañga kicked and cuffed the Hyena, and dragged her off, and said it was not thus Ndeba was to die. Then he called upon the young men, and they came up and took hold of Ndeba, and whilst some unwound the bush-rope that had bound her, others tied fresh ropes round her neck, ankles, and wrists, and with the ends of these ropes they lashed her round the trunk of the big tree. 'And is that all?' I asked of another of my father's wives, for I could not find my mother; 'are they not going to kill her?' 'No,' she replied, 'it is Epfumo who will kill her, but she will take some time to die, for she is strong even yet, although the Hyena has spoilt her face.' And all this time Ndeba said nothing, she was quite dumb, and did not seem to know what had happened. And, after she was tied to the tree, every one seemed to forget her, and the men and women had a big dance round the fire. Presently my mother came up to me and took me home, and I asked her where she had been all the time, and whether she had seen what had been done to Ndeba; and she said yes, she had seen all, but I did not believe that she was there. And the next morning there was a great clamour among the women in my father's yard, and the Hyena, who was now the head-wife, reproached my mother with her love for Ngwi, and threatened she would tell everything to my father, but my mother soothed her and hushed her and reminded her that the dead Ejok had been such a friend to me, and when my mother mentioned Ejok's name, the Hyena burst out crying, and promised not to say anything about Ngwi. And that day Ngwi sent my mother a large fish which he had caught in the river, and she divided the fish among all the other women, and they seemed to be great friends.

CHAPTER IV.

THE next day I went out with some of my brothers to snare birds in the forest, and when we were coming back in the evening we passed through the square where the people danced, and where the sacrifices used to take place, and there was Ndeba still tied to the tree; and when I went up to her, her eyes opened, and she looked at me, but she could not speak, because they had thrust a gag into her mouth. Just above her head they had driven into the tree a small peg, and on this was hung a bundle of red parrot-feathers; this meant that Ndeba was 'fetish;' that no one must touch her, or aid her, or give her food or water, or have anything to do with her, or Epfumo would kill them. So the other boys drew me away from staring at her, and we all went home with the birds we had caught.

And three days after that there was a big market held in the square, a market that took place in our town every ten days, and people came to this market from great distances when there was not war in the land: and here, for the first time, I saw a Ful merchant, a Mohammedan, who had come from the north to buy ivory and slaves. He had with him one or two people from a country near ours who had become the allies and servants of the Mohammedan Ful-be, and who dressed in long blue robes and turbans, like Mohammedans, and although I was frightened at first, and held on to mother's hand, still I looked at this man with wonder and curiosity; and I being then a pagan and one of the brutes of the field, wondered that this man should cover his body with cloth, for all the people of our town and country went naked except for their bracelets of ivory or their neck ornaments. And when I looked at the tree where Ndeba was

'We all went home with the birds we had caught.'

bound I saw to my surprise that she was still alive—that is to say, her eyes opened and shut as she watched the coming and going of the people, but they all took no notice of her, and none offered to give her food or water, or to loose her bonds.

Once the Pul-o merchant asked some questions about her, but the young men of the town said to him, 'It is our business, meddle not with her,' and he laughed and turned away.

The next day I thought much about Ndeba, and wondered whether she still lived, and whether her eyes could still open and shut. So, without telling my mother, who, I knew, would scold me, I slipped away from the yard alone, and stole to the square in the forest. Around the base of the tree were walking two or three brown vultures of a kind that were tame in our town, like fowls, for we allowed them to eat the offal, and no man might disturb them.

When I stepped as close as I might to Ndeba I saw that her eyelids had dropped. But when I said in a soft voice, 'Ndeba!' her eyes opened and she looked hard at me.

Wallah! it is wonderful how these old women live! Here she had been tied to the tree for six days, and was not dead yet. But I thought to myself as I ran back home, 'She will surely die soon, or the vultures would not be walking about her.'

And still the next day I thought about Ndeba, and wondered whether she was dead yet. But I feared to leave our compound early the next morning, because my mother had asked me many questions about where I had been the day before, and had told me that if I went anywhere near Ndeba she would hand me over to Epfumo. However, soon there arose a clamour in the yard, because the Hyena rushed out of my father's house where she had been taking his morning food, and said he was not there, and that he must have disappeared for some hours, because the fire was out, and they sought for him everywhere in the compound, but could not find him.

'Around the base of the tree were walking two or three brown vultures. . . .
When I said in a soft voice, "Ndeba!"
her eyes opened, and she looked hard at me.'

My mother laughed and said, 'Puh! He has found his strength again, that is all. Perhaps it was Ndeba that bewitched him, and now he has grown strong, and gone off to hunt or trade.'

And then all the other women began shouting at my mother, saying she had hidden him or killed him lest he should find out about Ngwi, and while they were making all this to-do, I slipped out of our compound, and ran off to the forest to see whether Ndeba was still living.

And when I got to the square, to my surprise I saw my father sitting down near Ndeba's feet, and leaning against the trunk of the tree, but a vulture was perched on Ndeba's shoulder, tearing the flesh off her cheeks; so it was clear she was dead.

And what do you think? my father was dead, too, and when I touched his body to awaken him, for I thought he was asleep, he rolled over on the ground. I was so frightened at this, fearing lest they should say I had killed him, that I ran right into the forest and hid there all the rest of the day, and at nightfall I re-turned home, hoping that they would not notice my absence, or would think that I had been to snare birds.

But long before I reached our compound I heard the wailing of the women, crying out for my father's death, for his body had been found in the marketplace, and brought back to our home. And my mother told me that Epfumo had killed my father, be-cause he had been to say good-bye to Ndeba.

The next morning, quite early, my mother caught her largest she-goat, one that had a little one running by her side, and a duck which she had bought from a Ful trader, and cut a big bunch of plantains out of her plantations. She set the bunch of plantains on my head, and made me carry the duck under one arm, and lead the goat with the other hand. Then she told me to go to the house of Asho-ntshofi, the Ñgañga, and say, 'This is a present from Tutu, the wife of Asho-eso.' Only that I was to say, and nothing more, and then to return as quickly as possible.

When I reached the Ñgañga's compound, there, too, was
Ngwi, the young man that was my mother's friend, and he had
with him two goats and a bag of kauri shells.[21] He went in before
me, and gave these things to the Ñgañga, with whom he had a
long talk which I could not hear. I was tired of waiting, so I
began to rummage among the rubbish which lay in the Ñgañga's
courtyard, and in one of the heaps of rubbish I remember I
picked up part of a man's jaw, which had the teeth still in it, although they were loose, and I pulled all the teeth out to make
myself a necklace, but whilst I was doing this the Ñgañga came
up, and cuffed me on the head for meddling with his treasures.

Then he asked my business, and I gave him my mother's message and the present she had sent. He bade me wait whilst he
went back into his house, and then he came out again with
some red feathers of a parrot and some string made of human
gut, which he told me to give to my mother, who was to hang
the feathers round her neck with the piece of string. When I
returned to our compound, my mother was waiting for me, and
took me aside and asked me in a whisper what the Ñgañga had
said, and I gave her the string and the parrot-feathers, and told
her what she was to do, at which she clapped her hands and
seemed pleased. When I went back with her into the courtyard
I saw the Hyena, who was the head-wife since Ndeba's death,
sitting on one of our native stools, whilst other women were
painting her all over with the camwood dye, and then drawing
lines of white, in a kind of pattern, round her eyes, down the
sides of her neck, and along the outer part of her arms. I ran to
my mother to know what they were decking the Hyena for, and
she said, with a laugh, that she was making herself smart for her
journey to the Under-world.

'Where is the Under-world?' I asked. 'Is it beyond the mountain, on the great river?'

'No,' she said, 'it is under the ground, where dead people

go when they are buried. Thy father has gone there, since Epfumo has called him, and now the Hyena must go too, to tend
upon him.'

That same day some of the young men from the town came
to prepare my father to be put into the earth. They opened his
body and took out his bowels, which they buried in the ground
in the middle of the compound; then they made a big fire in
the hut where my father lived, and after they had sewn up the
body they smoked it on a frame of sticks above the fire, and
there it lay all the rest of the day and the whole night, till it
was quite black and dry; and it got so small, so shrunken, that
it was not like my father at all. The next morning they took it
down off the sticks, and rubbed the smoke-black off with the
husks of bananas and with corn-cobs, so that the body was
shiny like leather. After this they got the red dye and white
earth, and painted the face of the corpse red and white, and
put on the ivory bracelets and the charms that my father had
worn round his neck when he was alive, and then they got the
grass-cloth which our people used to weave and dye red and
black, and they wound these cloths round and round his body,
so that it was like a bundle, and only the head was free: but before they wound this cloth round him they bent the legs up, so
that my father was sitting with his knees close to his chest, just
as he sat when he was alive, and when the cloth was wound
round and round his body, it kept the knees and the arms in
position. Then they dug a big, big hole in the floor of my father's hut.

And whilst this was going on, all that day the Hyena had
been led round about the town, painted up in the way I have
told you; she was led by the other wives of my father. She went
to all the people in the town to say good-bye, and each gave
her greeting, and many gave her presents to take with her. And
when all was ready, the grave dug, and the corpse prepared, they

sent for the Ñgañga, and all the people began to come to our compound, carrying torches, for it was night. Then some of my other brothers brought three white goats from my father's flock and three white fowls, and baskets of ground-nuts and maize. And the Ñgañga, who was painted all over in different colours and had a monkey-skin cap upon his head, began to dance round the grave, and said a lot of silly words which I did not understand. After this he called in a loud voice on my father, 'Asho-eso, art thou ready to go?' And, though no one answered, he pretended to listen at the lips of the corpse whom they had seated at the edge of the grave, and then he turned to the other people and said, 'I hear him say "Yes."' So the young men got bush-rope and tied it round the corpse and lowered it into the grave.

Then some one led up the Hyena. I could see that she was trembling very much, but she did not speak, and the Ñgañga bade her lie on the ground by the side of the grave. She lay down on her back, and he kneeled on her chest, got her neck in his skinny hands, and squeezed it so that she was strangled and died. Then they laid her body in the grave at the feet of my father. And after this they brought the three white goats and three white fowls and cut their throats one after another over the grave, so that the blood fell on the two corpses, but the bodies of the goats and fowls were taken away to be eaten at the funeral feast. The Ñgañga scattered a few of the ground-nuts and some maize into the grave, and they put in a horn of snuff and a wisp of salt in a banana leaf, and a gourd of water, some red peppers and some wooden dishes; and then the earth was all heaped back into the grave and trampled down by the young men. After this they had a big feast, and my mother gave me a large piece of meat. All the night they stayed singing and shouting and drinking palm-wine, until they were most of them drunk.

The next day all the big men met in the Epfumo house to say

'She set the bunch of plantains on my head, and made me carry the duck under one arm, and lead the goat by the hand.'

who should be the next chief, and some said one man and some said another, and whilst they were quarrelling the Ñgañga came dancing in, blowing his horn, and shouting out that he had a message from Epfumo, and the message was that Ngwi was to be the new chief.

Some grumbled at this, and said he was too young, but no one thought of disputing the Ñgañga's word. So the next day the Ñgañga gave to Ngwi my father's ebony staff, and Ngwi came down and took possession of our compound and all that was in it, and the three remaining wives of my father became the wives of Ngwi, and Ngwi made my mother the head-wife, so that she had all the other wives as her servants.

And Ngwi killed ten of my father's goats and tapped many palm-trees, so that there were great jars of palm-wine. And he dug up many yams and ground-nuts, and prepared a big feast, to which all the men of the village came. They were all pleased at this, and said Ngwi would make a good chief after all, because he was generous and fed the hungry. And I liked Ngwi, because he was kind to me and gave me a big ivory bracelet.

CHAPTER V.

AFTER my father's death several years went by, and things went well for our village. Ngwi was a brave man in war, and several times defeated the people of the mountain, bringing back with him many slaves and goats and sheep, and he made several new plantations, and dug cunning pitfalls for the elephant, so that our store of ivory increased. And he took four new wives, and begat children with them all. I learnt to shoot with the bow and arrow, and to hurl the dart with a good aim, and Ngwi promised me that when I should be made a man he would give me a gun, for at this time our people had begun to get guns from the Ful-be traders.

As I grew older I saw less of my mother, and as she had another child by Ngwi, she cared less for me, and would often drive me out of her hut impatiently when I came to her for food, and besides, I liked more to go out with the bigger boys fishing or hunting, or pretending to play at war with blunt arrows and wooden spears, which we used to aim at each other. They did not do much harm, as they had not sharp points, but one day I shot an arrow into a boy's eye and put out his sight. I was very proud of this, and Ngwi praised me, and said I should make a good warrior, but he had to pay a goat in compensation to the father of the boy.

Ngwi was very good to me, and used to take me with him sometimes, when he went on a trading expedition to a Ful settlement, two or three days distant from the village. Here I used to see the Mohammedans riding on horses and asses, animals that were new to our people, who always called them the 'white man's cows,' for as the Ful-be were so much lighter than we in

The Ndoge Brotherhood.

colour, we used to call them 'Pañ-mukwo,' or 'white men.'

One day Ngwi looked at me attentively, and said I was getting big enough to be made into a man, and soon after that the
old Ñgañga came to our compound and told me I must go away
with him. At the same time Ngwi had to pay him a goat, and
my mother gave him a small present too. Ngwi gave the goat
because, as he had taken our 'house,' he was looked upon as my
father; and, indeed, I believe he was so in reality. The Ñgañga
made me follow him to a place about an hour's walk from the
town, in the middle of the woods. It was a large enclosure, surrounded by a hedge of spiky-leaved plants, called 'Ngonje.' Inside were a number of huts, with a large Epfumo house in the
middle of the enclosure. As we went in a number of big boys,
as big and bigger than myself, rushed out of the little houses,
making a curious noise like 'Drrr,' and speaking to me in a
strange language, which I did not understand.

They were all clothed with a large skirt made of palm-leaves,
which was attached to their waists. Their bodies were covered
with red paint, and a lot of white marks were drawn about their
faces. When I had looked carefully into their eyes I recognised
first one and then another as old playfellows, who had disappeared from our village recently, and at the time I had asked
about their disappearance I was told that they were sent away
to be made into men. When I called them by their names they
were very angry and beat me with sticks, and the old Ñgañga
told me that I must not call them by their old names any more,
as they had changed them for new ones, and also that I must
not speak to them until I had learnt the sacred language, and
that every time I spoke in the old tongue the other boys would
beat me; that I must not eat this, or this, or this, until I was
made a man, or it would kill me, and the things that we were
allowed to have for our food were certain roots and fruits, which
we had to search for in the woods, and flesh of monkeys and

lizards and snakes, and any wild creatures which we could kill with our bows and arrows, but goat's-flesh, and fowls, and fish were forbidden to us. At first I was told that I must be a servant to the elder boys, and together with others who, like myself, had just been admitted, we had to prepare the food and cook for the bigger boys; and often these elder ones beat us, and the Ñgañga seldom interfered, saying that beating was good for the young.

Once when I forgot the rule about speaking in the common language, one of my companions hit me such a blow on the head with his club that for some time I did not know where I was, but the next day, when we were out hunting, I shot him in the back with an arrow, so that he was sick long afterwards, and this I said I would do to any one who struck me again; and after this the bigger boys did not treat me so harshly. When I had been eight days in this place, the medicine-man took me and some other younger boys, who had entered the enclosure about the same time as myself, and circumcised us.

After this we who had run naked hitherto made ourselves skirts of palm-fronds, and painted ourselves red and white, like the other boys. Now we were considered to be men, and we each received a new name. I, who had been called 'Mvu' hitherto (which means 'dog'), was named 'Mitwo,' which means 'Big Head.' And like the others I began to learn the new language, which was different from the one we commonly talked, though it was made chiefly by turning the words the wrong way: thus instead of 'Ñguo' (stone), we said 'Oñgu.' Sometimes in our walks abroad we met people of our town, and were told that if we spoke to any one who did not belong to the 'Ndoge'—as our brotherhood was called—Epfumo would kill us; moreover, we had the power to beat and wound any women who got in our way, and whenever we heard people approaching we always made the noise 'Drrr,' so that they might get out of our way. All this time the Ñgañga would visit us once a day and tell us many things, and hold with us much loose conversation that I may not repeat to you. Every now and then the bigger boys were leaving our enclosure and coming not back, and when I asked where they were gone, I was told that they had left for another place where they must learn the last things the Ñgañga had to teach them.

And when it came to my turn to go, the Ñgañga had a piece of goat's skin tied over my face, so that I could not see, and led me by the hand for some distance through the bush, telling me always that if I pushed aside the goat's skin and looked at the road I was going Epfumo would kill me, and at last we stopped, and he bade me go down on my hands and knees, and then pushed me through a narrow place between some branches, and when I got through he made me stand up and took the goat's skin off my eyes, and then I heard loud voices and girls' laughter, and when I looked round I saw many young girls painted with red and white, and with the palm-leaf skirts, and with them were some of the older boys who had left our enclosure. And at first I felt silly, for the girls laughed and jeered at me; but the medicine-man bade me be of good courage and heed not what they said, as I was now a man. And in this place I sojourned some twenty days, and when this time was over the Ñgañga again put the goat's skin over my face and led me away along devious paths for about the space of an hour. And then, when we had stopped, he removed the goat's skin from my face and said to me, 'Now go to this brook and wash all the red and white paint from thy body, and cast away thy skirt of palm-leaves. Then follow this path, and it will take thee back to the town, where thou canst return to thy father's house. Tell all that thou meetest that thy new name is "Mitwo." Speak no word of all that thou hast seen and done during these months that thou hast been in the Ndoge, or assuredly Epfumo will kill thee. And suffer that no man call thee by the name of thy childhood, or it will bring thee misfortune.' And after this I returned to the town and entered my father's compound, where my mother and Ngwi rejoiced greatly to see me back, and gave me a goat and plantains and groundnuts, wherewith to make a feast with my friends.

Wallah! how I have talked to you to-day! See, you are weary; you open your mouth in big yawns. I have said enough to-day. Let me go my way about my master's business, and I will come to you again in the morning.

CHAPTER VI.

WHEN I had returned from the Ndoge I was not allowed to live any longer in my father's compound, for it was not considered seemly for a young unmarried man to live among his father's wives. I had to take up my abode with the other young men of the town who were bachelors. We had a big compound to ourselves, but we were obliged to hunt and fish, and make plantations to supply ourselves with food.

And it was about this time that the Ñgañga instructed me as to the Epfumo Society, to which nearly all the young free men of the village belonged, and it was there that I learnt that the Epfumo was really a man dressed up, and not a devil; only we were sworn a solemn oath not to reveal this secret, so that the women and children and slaves might still be kept in awe of the Epfumo, whom they thought to be a strong devil that would be able to find out all secrets. And several times—I knew no better than the other pagans, and did as they did—have I dressed up as Epfumo with other young men of the Society, and lain in wait to catch women who were out of their houses after the Epfumo gong had sounded; and these we could do with as we pleased, and no one—not even their husbands—could say us nay; and, indeed, some of us hid women that we captured for a long time in a secret place we had made in the woods, and to them we always threatened that they would be surely killed by Epfumo if they should at any time reveal the names of those who had carried them off; and when we were tired of the women we would let them return to their homes, and knowing that they had been captured by the Epfumo, no one asked them questions or rebuked them for their absence.

And once we caught a slave on the road, who had not hidden himself at the sounding of the drum, and him we killed and ate—Wallah! we were but as the brutes—in the Epfumo house that same night, and the old Ñgañga man praised us for our dexterity.

Twice, whilst I was living with the other young men of the town, we were called upon to go to war with the Bakuba people of the mountain, a few days' distant from us. The first time we fought them because they had carried off a woman belonging to our town, and killed her husband, having surprised them on the way to trade with the Ful-be; and the second time Ngwi said we must attack the mountain people by stealth, and try to capture some of the women to sell as slaves to the Ful-be.

The first time I had to go to war I feared greatly, although the people called me 'Big Head,' because they thought me strong and courageous; but I was new to war, and feared to be killed and eaten by the mountain people, so that I did not adventure myself in the front of the party that attacked the Bakuba; but whilst I was skulking in the rear I espied a Bakuba man and woman who had been out cutting grass for their goats, and whom our attack had cut off from the town. They sought to escape our notice by crawling on their stomachs through the grass like snakes, and winding behind every rock and stump till they should arrive close to the Bakuba stronghold; but seeing they were unarmed, save for the small cutlass which the man had, I attacked them suddenly as they were lying on the ground, drove my spear right through the man's body and pinned him to the ground, and knocked the woman down with my club. Then my heart grew big, and I shouted loudly to my comrades to tell them what I had done, and some of them came running up and cut off the head of the man through whom I had run my spear, and helped me to tie the arms and ankles of the woman before she awoke.

'I espied a Bakuba man and woman who had been out cutting grass for their goats. . . . .
They sought to escape our notice by crawling on their stomachs through the grass like snakes.'

The rest of our party did not do much against Bakuba, because they found the town well defended and few of its fighting
men were absent; so after they had shouted much, and shot
many arrows, and called the Bakuba every foul name they could
think of to draw them from their stockade, Ngwi and my companions decided to retreat. So we returned to our town with
the body of the man I had killed and the woman I had captured,
and my mother shrieked loudly with joy when they told her
what a brave man her son had become. The body of the man
we warriors ate in the Epfumo house, and good and sweet was
the flesh—Wallah! it is shameful that I say such things now,
but *Alhamdu'lillah!* I am no longer a pagan and an eater of man's
flesh—and the woman I had captured I took to wife, and made
work in my plantations. My mother said to me, 'Treat her well,
and she will remain with thee, but if thou hast the heart to use
her badly, it were better to sell her to the Batibari[22] than to let
her remain in our town, for if she is unhappy she will surely find
a way to escape back to her country.'

So I said to the woman, 'Wilt thou swear by Epfumo to stay
with me, and be a true wife to me?' and she replied, 'My heart
is sad for having left my country, but thou art the strongest.
Thou killedst my man—what other man have I now to love beside thee? I will swear by Epfumo not to leave thee if thou treat
me kindly.' We sent for the Ñgañga, and he brought the 'ju-ju'
mixture, which is made of man's flesh and drugs from the woods,
and he put some of this on the tongue of my woman: she, putting one hand on her head and the other hand in mine, swore
that she would remain with me and become one of our people.
After this I got my friends to help me, and we built a house and
made a yard for me to live in, for I was now a married man, and
dressed my hair in the fashion of those who were married men.

The second time we went to war with the Ba-kuba was, as I
have said, to capture women to sell to the Ful-be. For when my

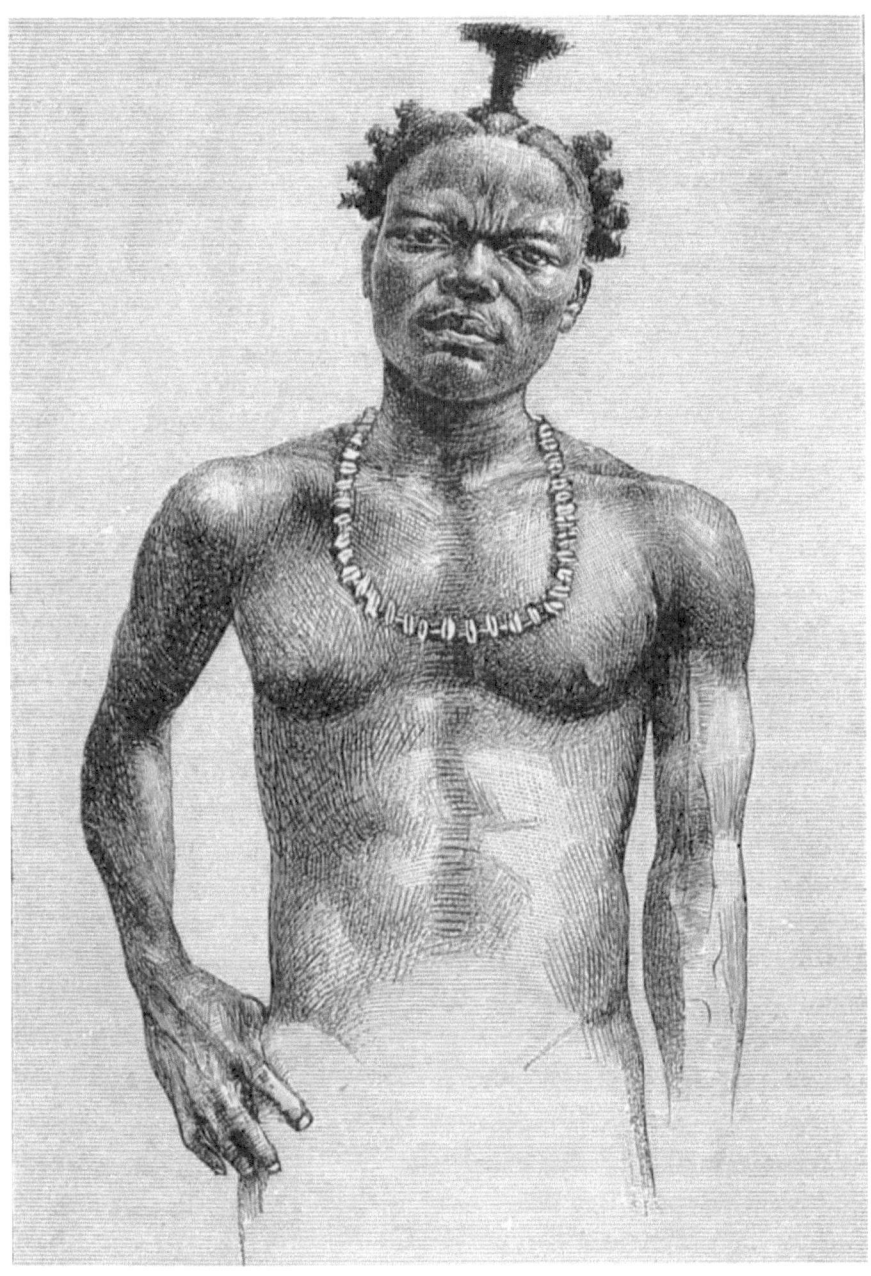

'I dressed my hair in the fashion of those who were married men.'

'As the elephants, scared by the torches and the shouting, pressed onwards between the narrow hedges, some of them were pushed into the pit and were at the men's mercy.'

wife had grown to know me and like me, she told me one day
that about the night when it should be full moon it was the
custom of the men among her people to leave the town and
surround the plantations, where the elephants came to rob
them, and that they had fashioned two great hedges of sticks
and thorns which narrowed to a small lane, at the end of which
was a big, big pit, and that when they had surrounded the plantations that the elephants were rifling, they began with great
shouting and the flames of their torches to drive the elephants
into the space between the two hedges that converged in the
pit, and that as the elephants, scared by the torches and the
shouting, pressed onwards between the narrow hedges, some of
them were pushed into the pit and were at the men's mercy; for
the elephant in some things is a foolish beast, and has not the
wit to turn aside and break through the fence of thorns, but
presses on towards the outlet where the pit awaits him.

And when I told all this to Ngwi he considered awhile, and
said: 'I have a good plan in my head: let us select all the strong
and valiant among the men of this town two days before the
moon is full, and let us journey secretly through the bush until
we are close to the Bakuba town, on the mountain. Then we
will lie concealed in the woods among the stones, and await
the time when we shall see the men of the town issuing forth
with their torches to hunt the elephants. And when they are
away in the plantations we will take the town by surprise, and
capture as many of the women as we can secure quickly, and
having done this we will return to our town with what speed
we can.'

This we did, and brought back with us it might be thirty, it
might be forty, women and a few young children. We had captured many more, but the Bakuba men pursued us and harried
us on our return, and recovered some of their people, although
in their fighting they themselves lost nine or ten men whose

bodies we ate on our return. And of our town four men only were killed in battle, for Ngwi was cunning, and knew how to skillfully direct the fighting. And as the bodies of these four were carried off by the Bakuba, and therefore could not be buried, the Ñgañga said that none of their wives need follow them to the Under-world, inasmuch as the bodies of their husbands rested doubtless in the stomachs of the Bakuba; and this was said to be a wise word, and the men of the town applauded when the Ñgañga divided the wives of the slain amongst those who had been bravest in the battle. And as I pleased the Ñgañga by my prowess I received one of these women for a wife; and, moreover, I had kept back for myself a young girl whom I had captured in the Bakuba country, so that I had now three wives and became a big man in the town.

CHAPTER VII.

BUT what we had done against the Bakuba was surely bad in Allah's sight, for He made it a means of bringing about our punishment.

When the day came round for the next big market to be held in our town—the market that we used to have every ten days— there were more of the Mohammedan, Ful, and Hausa traders there than we had ever seen before. They had heard that we had some new slaves to sell; and about this time, too, from the number of elephants that the young men began to kill, we had a large store of ivory to trade with; all of which Ngwi made us sell for guns and gunpowder, for he was determined that we should become so strong that the Bakuba people should no longer be able to fight with us, and should come under our power altogether.

One of these Mohammedan traders, whose name was Rashidu, talked to me much about the Sultan of Gashka,[23] and asked me how our people would like to become Mohammedans, and live under the Sultan of Gashka's rule. I told him—foolish pagan as I was—that we liked best to worship the spirits of our fathers, and to follow in their ways; and that, although the Sultan of Gashka might be a strong and just man, we would sooner live under our own chiefs.

This man asked me many questions about our country and the countries beyond us to the south; and he told us, if we went many days' journey towards the setting sun, we should come to the great water where the white people ruled. He also said that he liked so much the slaves he had bought at this market that we must wage other wars on our neighbours, and get more and

'When the day came round for the next big market to be held in our town . . . there were more of the Mohammedan, Ful, and Hausa traders there than we had ever seen before.'

more slaves; so that when he came again, in three months' time, he would find a good number of slaves ready for sale. He talked to me in the Juku[24] language, which I partly understood from the trading journeys which I had made.

When the market was over, and the Ful-be traders had left our town with their slaves, and asses, and the ivory they had bought, I reported to Ngwi all that Rashidu had said to me. When he heard these words he shook his head and said he liked them not; he had heard that a country not far away from us, called Banyo,[25] had lately been ravaged by this same Sultan of Gashka, and many of its people carried off into slavery. What if the Ful-be of Gashka should do the same to us?

But I, not knowing the strength of people beyond our borders, laughed at Ngwi's words, and said, 'And if they do come and fight, have we not also guns now, and would we not fight for our homes and our women?'

A matter of some three months slipped by, and nothing troubled us; but we had not got the number of slaves we had hoped to obtain, because we had made friends with the Bakuba people of the mountain. It was such Bakuba people as we had among us as slaves and wives that urged us to do this, and Ngwi was of opinion that it was foolish for this fighting always to go on. Moreover, the Bakuba people agreed that, if we swore an oath not to attack them any more, they would consent to accept Ngwi as their head chief, and many of the elders in both Bahom and Bakuba were of opinion that it was time we made up our quarrels and became as brothers; for, they said, 'We hear news from the north that the "Pañ-mukwo"[26]—the Ful-be chiefs who worship Allah—are extending their rule in all directions, and are enslaving the black men, the people of the land. It is time, therefore, we black people were united against them.'

And, when we were all agreed upon this, we sent messages to the Dokaka and Jetem[27] peoples to the east and south of us,

'They said that along the horizon in the direction of Dokaka they saw the smoke of burning towns.'

telling them what we had done, and asking them to join with us in resisting the Batibari, as we used to call the Ful-be Mohammedans. And they consented to this. And the chief of the Dokaka sent one of his daughters to wed with Ngwi, so that the two peoples might become more surely friends. But all this availed nothing against the decrees of Allah, as I will further relate to you.

After, as I think, some three months had passed since the Ful-be traders had come to buy our Bakuba slaves, our great trouble came upon us. One day some of our young men, who had been two days' journey to the east to trade with the Dokaka, came back to our town breathless with much running, and exhausted with want of food. When they had got their speech, they told us that the King of Gashka had sent a great army, some on foot and many riding on horses and asses, which had suddenly entered the Dokaka country and wasted it in all directions, burning the town, shooting the fighting-men, and catching the young women and children for slaves; and added that, having eaten up Dokaka, it was likely that the Gashka warriors would attack us and the Bakuba.

At these words we were filled with consternation, and Ngwi sent some of the young men to creep stealthily through the grass and forest till they reached the high hill which was a short distance from our town in the direction of Dokaka, and he told them to climb to the top of this hill, and to look out in the direction whence the other young men had come, and report whether they saw anything to bear out their statements. At eventide these spies returned, and terror was in their faces, for they said that along the horizon in the direction of Dokaka they saw the smoke of burning towns, and one whose eyes were sharper than the rest thought he could distinguish men dressed in long clothes riding on horseback across the plain. Then did we lay our heads together, that we might make preparations for defence. The women and children were all sent to Bakuba, as being a place more easy to defend, and we men remained behind in the town, sending our spies out into the forest and on to the hills in all directions, to keep us apprised of the advance of the Ful-be.

But we had begun our precautions too late. The women, who feared to start at night on account of the wild beasts and ghosts, of which these pagans are always afraid, left the village to escape to Bakuba just before the dawn; but before the sun was up they came running back into the town, shrieking out that the men riding on horses were upon us; and then our scouts came in one after the other, some wounded with the enemy's bullets, and all said, 'The Batibari are here! There is no time to escape!' And all was hubbub and confusion. Some went and hid themselves, some began to load their guns and get ready their spears and arrows, others cut down branches from the trees and tried to block the doorways of the different compounds; but there was great panic and confusion everywhere, and although Ngwi shouted, and ordered, and tried to assemble the fighting-men together, every one seemed to go his own way, and think only of securing his own property.

In the middle of all this turmoil we heard suddenly the firing of guns and distant shouting of 'Allah Akbaru,' the war-cry of the Ful-be; and then, as it were, all at once the town was full of Mohammedans, some on foot, and some crashing through the plantations on horseback; and our people ran hither and thither like frightened sheep. But there was no escape, for the Ful-be had surrounded the town, and any who tried to slip past the enemy into the bush were shot down. Six of the Ful-be, with guns and cutlasses, came into my compound, and I was afraid to resist them, for I saw it was useless to fight against them. But a little slave boy, whom I had captured from the Bakuba, aimed at them an arrow from his little bow, and they in rage seized him and blew out his brains. And then telling us that if we moved we should be likewise slain, they proceeded to bind my three wives and myself, by chaining our ankles together, and fastening us one to the other round the neck with other chains, and tying our hands behind us. When this was done five of them marched us out of the compound into the open space in front, where we saw others of my country-people also chained and fettered, and sitting or lying in groups.

Round these captives were standing a ring of Ful-be and Hausa warriors, with their guns loaded, and ready to shoot any who might try to escape or resist. There was an incessant wailing of the women and children. Among these I saw my mother, who, in between her cries, told me that Ngwi was killed: that he had fought desperately, and had killed two of the Ful-be, after which they had managed to knock him down with a club, and had cut his head off.

Whilst half the Ful-be guarded us, whom they had chained, the other part of the army was ranging through the town, some of the soldiers searching for hidden slaves, and laying hands on all the goats and sheep and ivory they could find, and others being sent to prevent any of our people from lurking concealed.

Presently a great cry arose from among the Ful-be that were standing guard over us. I could not understand what they were saying, because they spoke in their own language, which I did not then know; but it appeared as I afterwards learnt that some of our people, who at the first alarm had escaped into the bush, had set on two of the Ful-be whom they had found separated from their companions, and looting some plantations, and had killed them, and this aroused the wrath of the other Ful-be to such an extent that we feared they would kill us all. They captured most of the runaway party who had been concerned in the death of their brothers, and brought them into the open place where we were lying chained. Not a few of these runaways

were poor women and little children, who could not have had
anything to do with the death of the two Ful-be soldiers; but,
nevertheless, on them as well as on their husbands and brothers
the Mohammedans wreaked their anger.

They tied the men to stakes and tree trunks, and lopped their
limbs off one by one, and then beheaded them; they ripped up
the women, and lifting up the children by the feet they swung
them round and dashed out their brains on the stone seats in
the open square, where our elders used to sit under the shade
of the big trees. Then their leader spoke to us in the language
of Mbum,[28] which most of us understood (for it was the language of trade), and told us that if any of us attempted to stir
hand or foot from where we were laid, the same punishment
should be meted out to us. Whilst these things were being done
a small body of the Ful-be were busy burning the town, and cutting down the plantations of bananas, and setting fire to the
dry bush outside the town, so that the whole place might be
laid bare and afford no hiding-place to such of our people as
might have escaped, and think of lurking near the Ful camp.

All through that day, some in the sun and some in the shade,
we lay chained together in the open square of our town. One
or two of the women who were far gone with child died from
the fright and the anguish of their premature delivery, and so
we lay all through the night, while the Ful-be made big bonfires
and roasted our sheep and goats.

CHAPTER VIII.

EARLY the next morning they passed in review all of us whom they had captured, which I suppose amounted to one-half of our townspeople—perhaps some five hundred. They made us stand up in our chains—men, women, and children (the little children were not chained, because the Ful-be knew they would not leave their mothers)—and we were carefully examined by the leader of the Ful soldiers. All such as were aged, or deformed, or weakly were separated from the others, and put on one side. Their chains were taken off, and they were told jestingly by the Ful-be that they might go where they pleased; but when the poor simpletons began to slink off towards the bush, the Ful-be, with shouts of laughter, began firing at them with their guns and riding them down on horseback.

Some of the Ful-be horsemen would stop for a moment and tie a rope round the ankle of one of these fugitives who had fallen down, and fasten the other end of this rope to his stirrup, and then ride round and round the square at full gallop, till the man he had dragged with him was simply a shapeless mass of blood and bones.

At length their leader recalled all his men by having a drum beaten, and orders were given to get ready for a start.

All we slaves whom they had selected to take away with them were marched in twos and threes to the river, where we were made to wash and drink. Here several who were mad with grief jumped into the river, though they were chained together, and tried to swim down the stream, but they all sank to the bottom and were seen no more.

One woman, who had been incessantly howling all the

'Some of the Ful-be horsemen would tie a rope round the ankle
of one of these fugitives and fasten the other end of this rope to his stirrup,
and then ride round and round the square at full gallop.'

morning because her son had been killed by the Ful-be, was ordered several times by those who were guarding us to cease her
noise, and as she paid no heed to their warning, she was shot.
After we had been made to drink at the river we were ranged
in a row on the bank, and the Ful-be distributed among us food
from our own plantations. This we were ordered to eat, and
threatened with immediate death if we refused.

About mid-day the Ful-be army was got into order, and the
slaves were made to march in the centre of the caravan, with
soldiers in front and behind, some widening the road as we went
along—that is to say, cutting down the bush to prevent any enemies concealing themselves on the line of route. All of us
slaves who were men had our hands securely tied behind our
backs with coils of bush-rope, and round our necks were fastened slave-sticks, linking every two slaves together. The
women's hands were free, so that they might more easily take
their children with them, either by holding their hands or carrying them slung round their back. In this fashion we walked
all the rest of that day, and slept at night in a Ful-be camp,
where we found a lot more Mohammedan soldiers of the King
of Gashka who had been slave-raiding at Bakuba, and had
brought back with them a number of Bakuba people whom they
had captured.

The next day the whole force set out, with all the soldiers,
to travel to a large town called Banyo, which we reached in four
days' time. Any slaves that could not keep up with the march
of the caravan were stabbed or shot, and left behind, and the
fear of this death made us walk as we had never walked before.
But with some of the women who were young and comely the
Ful-be soldiers were not so harsh, and would occasionally
mount them on the asses that carried the camp-baggage. In this
way I saw that two of my wives had already made friends with
their guardians, and one of them was even laughing when the

'I saw her body . . . cast out into the street, where the hyenas which wander through the town at night came and tore it to pieces.'

soldiers jested—so soon do these poor pagans forget. On the road, every night we stopped to camp, the Ful-be gave us just as much food as would keep us from starving; but those who were young and well made got a little more than those who were old and ungainly. Thus my mother, who was getting on in years, and was worth little as a slave, received such scant food from the Ful-be that the fatigue of these four days' journey caused her to die of weakness soon after we got to Banyo; and, as I lay joined to another man in the market-place at night, I saw her body released from its bonds by the soldiers and cast out into the street, where the hyenas which wander through the town at night came and tore it to pieces.

Banyo is a big town belonging to the Sultan of Gashka. It is a place where the pagans of many nations, who are more or less under the Pul-o rule, bring their ivory and slaves for sale. I saw men here from many far countries, whose speech I could not understand. When we had rested several days at Banyo we again set out for Gashka, which we reached after about two days' journey, passing a big mountain on the way. Along this road not a few of the slaves sank down from weariness and were killed, for the road we followed was very arduous, lying among hills and valleys and great rocks. When we reached Gashka I was so tired that I cared not whether I lived or died. But here we were a little better treated by the Ful-be.

Before we got into the town the Sultan came out with a lot of his soldiers on horseback to meet this army which he had sent slave-raiding, and he was mightily pleased at the number of slaves they had obtained. There was a great firing of guns, and shouting, and blowing of horns, and 'lalilu-ing' on the part of the Ful-be women, who shrieked out all manner of jests at us as we went by, calling out many words about our nakedness, which caused them to laugh. When we got into the town we slaves were divided into small companies and distributed among the principal men of the town, who were to keep us in watch and ward till the Sultan should decide what to do with us. By great good fortune I found myself with my head-wife and one of my brothers and five other people of our town. Much we wept together for the sorrows that had overtaken us.

The man to whom we were entrusted was none other than the commander of the expedition, and him we found a not unkindly master. We were taken into his courtyard, and he explained to us in the Mbum language that he should take off our fetters, so that we should be free to walk about his compound, but if we attempted to escape we should be killed at once; 'and, moreover, if we did get outside the town, where were we to go? We were now many days' journey from our country, which had been laid waste, and wherever we might wander we should find the Ful-be there ready to recapture us.' Then, according to our country fashion, he made us take a pinch of the soil between our fingers and swear not to run away, and this, seeing no help for it, we did, and after so doing our lot was less hard, for we were allowed to wash ourselves, and could eat and drink in plenty.

After we had stayed in Gashka perhaps ten or twelve days, a big slave market was held there, at which nearly all the slaves which the Ful-be had captured in their recent raids were exposed for sale, and a Pul-o slave merchant from Yola,[29] after closely examining me, bought me for two thousand kauri shells, and he also purchased five other of our people, among whom was my head-wife. Our new master joined himself to a big Ful caravan, with which he travelled to Yola during many days over a mountainous country that was inhabited by the Kotofo[30] people, who are friends of the Ful-be. On our way we passed on the west of a big, big mountain, bigger than any I had yet seen, and we reached Yola after spending twenty days on the road. When I beheld this place I was filled with wonder, for I had seen no

'On our way we passed on the west of a big, big mountain.'

town like it. It is not worthy to be compared with Tarabulus, nor with Kano or Murzuk or the great cities of the Sudan, but it far surpassed anything I had seen in my own country, and I began to think that after all we pagans were as monkeys compared to the Ful-be, and I felt ashamed that I was naked and had no clothes to make me look like a Mohammedan. On our journey to Yola I had won the favour of my Pul-o master, who was pleased to find me strong and active and good-tempered, and when we arrived at Yola he gave me an old blue cotton shirt to wear, with which I was greatly pleased, though he and his friends laughed much to see the way in which I at first wore it, for we pagans recking little of decency would have it that clothes should be worn to make a man look smart and not to cover his body, so that when I first got this shirt I wound it round my neck and shoulders until I was taught its proper use.

CHAPTER IX.

WHILE I stayed in Yola I began to learn the Ful language, or as those people call it the 'Fulful-de,' and when my master, the Pul-o merchant, found that I was of a mind to learn, be began to show me favour, and entrusted me with matters of trade rather than with labour in the plantations, such as the other slaves were put to. In this way I went with him on several small journeys into the Batta country, and to the great Pul-o town of Ribago;[31] and seeing that I was versed in the knowledge of the ivory traffic he employed me to choose out and buy tusks from the people round the big mountain—I think its name was Alantika[32]—and once I went as far as Ngaundere,[33] where we bought much ivory, and where my master gathered in many more slaves from the pagan countries round. Many of these were wild people, wilder than we had been in Mbudikum; most of them were stark naked, but some wore leaves, and we who were now clothed and had forgotten the days when we were pagans, laughed at these bushmen, and when they were handed over to our charge to carry the ivory, we treated them as the slaves of slaves, and beat them when they did not understand our orders.

When my master had collected a good supply of ivory and slaves he decided to set out from Yola, and proceed to a great city of the Ful-be called Yakuba,[34] in the country of Bautshi. This he told me was his home, and here he had a big house and many wives, and he was resolved to return thither, and after he had disposed of his slaves and ivory, to settle down with his women and children for the rest of his days. So when he had finished his business in Yola, and had given a handsome present

'He laughed much to see the way in which I at first wore it.'

to the Pul-o governor of that place, he trafficked with the Batta people, and bought many canoes, all of which, as is the fashion of these countries, were hollowed out of a single tree, and not put together with boards and nails as are the ships of the Arabs and the Christians, or even the boats of the fishing people that live round the Great Lake. And we loaded these canoes with the ivory which our master had collected. In charge of each canoe was put a trustworthy slave, and the ivory was weighed and counted, and written in a book, so that if any tusks were lost or stolen our master would surely find out and punish the slave who had been in charge of the canoe. And in the biggest canoe we put together a little house of palm-thatch which should be a place for our master to sit in, protected from the sun and rain; and when the canoes were all packed and the slaves all tied together and stowed away in them, we started on our journey down the great Benue, to reach the place called Wusu.[35]

Now it was the season of the rains, and the river was greatly risen in volume, and overflowed its banks for a considerable distance on either side, so that the water seemed like a great sea without limits, except for the deleb palms which rose above the flood, and marked where the borders of the stream should be in the dry season. Here and there we could see distant hills which looked like islands in a great lake. Many difficulties encompassed us in this journey, and often we were near to destruction, for the floods of the river having extended so far, it was exceedingly difficult for us to know which should be the right channel of the river, and hard to tell how we should avoid the great snags and fallen trees which lay concealed so near the surface of the water, and against which the canoes would often bump, so that we were near capsizing.

And worse than this were the river-horses—'Nseshe,'[36] as we used to call them in our country—animals as big almost as elephants, who live in the water and have great mouths stuck with

'The water seemed like a great sea without limits, except for the deleb palms which rose above the flood.'

huge teeth—and these 'Nseshe,' these river-horses, as the Arabs
call them, are of a bold and ferocious nature in the rainy season,
for it was the time of year when they were breeding, and whenever they could find a canoe in the shallow waters they would
often make for it and endeavour to upset it, either by bumping
the canoe underneath with their big heads, so that they stove
a hole in the bottom, or else seizing the gunwale with their
teeth and dragging the canoe over to one side and so capsizing
it. And, although my master gave orders that we should fire
many guns at these river-horses and hurl spears at them, this
did not secure us altogether from their pursuit; and, indeed, it
caused them sometimes to wax more fierce, and in this way we
lost two canoes and much ivory, for the river-horses broke their
sides in, and caused the ivory to fall into the river-mud, where
most of it was buried and lost, and the slaves that were in these
canoes, being thrown into the water, had to swim for their lives.
One of them was killed by a river-horse, who bit his body in
two; others were dragged down by crocodiles, and we saw them
no more. Two of them, who were women, our master took into
his own canoe. But the others, the men, he would not stay to
help, because the other canoes were already overcrowded, and
these slaves being of little value, he cared not to run any further
risk by picking them up. So what became of them I know not:
perchance they swam on until they touched ground and were
able to wade to the dry land, or it may be the crocodiles caught
them all.

For some time, as we paddled down stream, we could see
their heads bobbing like black points on the waste of waters,
and we laughed much when, every now and then, we heard a
scream, and guessed that a crocodile had seized another slave.
And we slaves, who cared little for the loss of the ivory, for it
was not ours, began to make many merry jests about the crocodiles, saying that they would thank Allah for the feast He had

given them; but our master, who was sad for the loss of his ivory, chide us and bade us be silent, or he would throw us to the crocodiles too.

In some places that we passed by there had been great floods, owing to the heavy rains; and, in the country of Basama,[37] the villages were all on little islands, with the water coming close up to the houses, and only the tops of the plantain trees showing here and there where the plantations were covered. And on one of these islands, where the village had been deserted by the inhabitants, who had fled away in canoes, we saw a strange sight. There was a lion seated on his haunches, a company of baboons on the roofs of the houses, some hogs, of a kind called 'Ngena' in our country language; two bush-deer, of a sort which we name 'Ngaba,' red-coated, with white stripes; and a large black snake, of a kind whose name is 'Nok' in Mbudikum, and which the Ful-be call 'Modondi.' And all these creatures, which are wont to disagree in the forest—the lion to eat the bush-deer, and the snake to eat the baboons, and the hogs to kill the snake—were now so scared by the flood, which had driven them for refuge to this small village on a little mound, that they looked not at each other, but watched the water only, as it mounted higher and higher, and ate up the ground as it rose; and our master bade us fire our guns and hurl our lances at the lion. But whether we killed him or not I cannot say, for the flood was so strong that we dare not turn the canoes broadside and stop, lest they should be overwhelmed. And, as we got nearer towards the district of Muri,[38] the great expanse of water grew less in breadth, for the mountains closed in nearer to the course of the stream; but, on this account, the force of the current grew even stronger.

At length the Pul-o soldier, who was one of my master's servants, called out to the steersman of the canoe that was leading to enter a small creek or branch of the river which appeared on our right-hand, and here the water was quieter, and soon after we had entered this narrow branch we stopped at a riverside town called Wuzu. Here all the slaves and the ivory were disembarked, and we all left the canoes, which were afterwards sold by our master to a Pul-o who lived at Muri.

At Wuzu my master only stayed sufficient time to get all the caravan in order, and then set out for Muri, which was a day's journey from Wuzu. Muri was a big town of the Ful-be, which belonged to the Sultan of Yakuba, and here my master had many friends and abode for several days, conversing with them; and here he bought many camels, and asses, and horses, with some of his ivory, and the rest of the tusks he packed on the camels and asses; and he resolved to sell at Muri, where there was a great market, most of his slaves, for he desired to proceed quickly to Yakuba, and no longer needed the slaves to carry the ivory. I feared that he would sell me here, for several Ful-be merchants examined me, and pinched my muscles, and said they liked the looks of me, but my master said that he would keep me for his own household, as I had a good head for trade, and a manner of saying things which caused him to laugh.

So when all was ready for our journey to Yakuba, my master bade me seat myself on one of those asses which had a load of ivory on its back; and at first I was greatly afraid, for I had never ridden any beast before, and the ass seemed to know that I was a pagan, for when I tried to mount him he would rear up his hind-quarters and throw off the ivory. At length I managed to get on, and although I slipped off several times over the ass's tail, I was vexed when my master jeered at me, and so I clung on with one hand clutching the ass's mane, and with the other holding one of his ears, and every time he would rear up before or behind, I would put the tip of his ear in my mouth and bite it, and he soon gave over trying to unseat me; and by the time we reached near to Yakuba I could ride without fear, and would

even at times mount on one of the camels, which were strange
beasts in my sight, for there was nothing like them in our
country.

When we had got within one day's journey of Yakuba we saw
the great mountains behind which the town lay, and my master,
with some of his friends and guards, rode on in front of the caravan, carrying with him a present for the 'Lamido,' or Sultan,
of the country, and bidding his head man, or overseer of slaves,
to lead us all by other roads to his plantations outside the town,
so that his wealth of ivory and slaves might not be shown to
the people of Yakuba (for it was said the Sultan of Yakuba was
a very greedy man, and harassed those whom he knew to be
rich); and so we abode several days at the plantations, where
the ivory was stored, and then one day my master came riding
out of the town to see that everything was safely stowed away,
and he chose out such slaves among us as he wanted (myself
among the number), and took us back with him into the town.

And here I was amazed at what I saw, for although Yola was
a big town, and the governor of it had a great house, and there
were one or two large mosques, there was nothing there that
could compare with Yakuba. The people of that place are more
in number than those of Tarabulus or Murzuk, and perhaps it is
only surpassed in populousness by Kano; though I have heard
the city of Sakatu[39] is a vast place inhabited by many people.
But to me, who was then a pagan and a bushman, Yakuba
seemed the grandest place in all the world, with its fine houses
of clay, and their wooden doors and arches and window-frames,
and its 'dakakin' (shops),[40] the like of which I had never seen
before. Here were merchants from as far as the Great Desert,
and even Ghadames, and people from Bornu and Sakatu and
Nufe. Some were selling the cloth made by the Christians,
which had reached even our country of Mbudikum from the
lands of Diwala[41] and the great sea. Others trafficked in the blue

'And all these creatures, which are wont to disagree in the forest . . .
were now so scared by the flood, which had driven them for refuge
to this small village on a little mound, that they looked not at each other,
but watched the water only.'

cloth of Nufe or the taubs of Kano, or sold leather sandals, finely embroidered, or saddles and horse-gear from the Hausa lands, or the white salt brought up the Kwara river in big ships by the Christians, and wonderful things of glass, and plates of earthenware and brass. And I tapped my mouth with amazement to think that the hands of men could fashion such things. And in one 'dukkan'[42] they were selling paper to write on, and reed pens and ink, and the Quran bound in leather—the book of Our Lord Mohammed, *Salam 'ala- Rasulnawa Nabina*—peace be upon our Apostle and Prophet! When I first saw these Qurans being sold I recked not of their value, for I was still a pagan, and I wondered to myself that men should give for them many kauri shells or great silver riyalat (dollars),[43] or a small tusk of ivory, seeing that these books were, to my ignorance, but made of leather and paper, and could neither be eaten nor burned for perfume, nor used for any purpose useful for man's body. And in another shop was an old Pul-o 'm'alam,' who was selling small pieces of sheep-skin, on which he had written something with a reed pen. And as my master stopped to buy one of these I asked him what their purpose was, and he said they were charms to be folded up and put in a small case which was made out of the shell of a nut, and to be hung round a man's neck, to avert any harm that might happen to him by evil spirits or to cure him of some malady. And if, perchance, a man was sick, there was no better medicine for him than to soften one of these pieces of sheep-skin in water, when it had been written on by the m'alam, and to swallow it, for the words thereon written were the words of our Lord Mohammed from the holy Quran, and were apt for the healing of both body and soul. Afterwards I came to know these things well, and many a time, Wallah! have my bodily ailments been cured by swallowing these charms, *Alhamd-'lillah!* And yet other 'dakakin' sold sweet perfumes—pastilles to burn in the house and to make a grateful

'Yakuba seemed the grandest place in all the world, with its fine houses of clay . . . and its dakakin (shops).'

'In this court the camels and horses of my master were tethered, and there were many ducks and fowls, and a few sheep.'

odour, or ointments wherewith a man's skin should be rubbed so that it glistened, and was sweet and pleasing in the nostrils of his friends. And so, passing through this great bazaar, we arrived at the courtyard of my master's house.

And what happened after this I must tell you on another occasion, for my tongue has wagged too much to-day. Besides, yesterday I had trouble with my master after I had remained so long with you, for he was vexed, and told me that his business suffered by my useless talking with you. If you want me again, you must make it all right with Si Abd-al-Ghirha, so that he may not oppose my coming to you. *Insh' Allah ushufka al-ghodwa*—God grant that I see you to-morrow. If you gave me a silver riyal I should return with a glad heart and a new turban, for it is not fitting that I should talk to a great Nasrani[44] with an old, dirty head cloth like this. *Allah yasalimk!*

CHAPTER X.

AYA! And must I go on telling you still the events of my life? Are you not weary of all this talk, talk, talk? It is strange how all the little things I have seen and done come back to my memory as I sit and converse with you. Think not that I am telling you lies. I speak the truth. *Allah yashud!*—may God bear witness! What was I saying yesterday, when I left off? Was I telling you about my Pul-o master, old Nyebbu? Yes, now I remember, I was speaking of his house.

This was a place built much in the fashion of the Arabs in Murzuk or Tarabulus, only not so fine because it was nearer to the land of the pagans, and moreover, like all our houses in the Blacks' country, it was built of clay, not stone. We passed through a narrow door opening on to the street, and came into a big courtyard, round which ran a high clay wall. Inside the courtyard were two or three tamarind trees and sycamores, under which there was a refreshing shade. In this court the camels and horses of my master were tethered, and there were many ducks and fowls and a few sheep. On the other side of the court, opposite to where we had entered, was a high wall which screened the house beyond, and another archway in the middle of the wall which was closed with a great wooden door. This my master pushed open, and led me after him into his diwan, a large cool room with small windows high up, and seats of clay running all round the sides, on which tanned goat-skins and handsome carpets and silk cushions were placed.

My master instructed me as to my duties, which were to attend on himself, to prepare his snuff, or his pipe, and to make his coffee or his *tshai* (tea), which he bought from the Maghrabi merchants, and to run his errands, and to keep his diwan clean. When he was laid down to rest and had fallen to sleep in the heat of the day, I stood up on the clay couches and looked through the small windows near the top of the walls, and through these I could see into the inner court of the house which belonged to the harim of my master, where his wives and women slaves dwelt.

Now the Ful-be, although they are Muslemin, are not jealous of their women as are the Arabs, neither are the women allowed as much freedom as they were in our country of Mbudikum, so that whereas my master was displeased if I entered the court and part of the house set apart for his harim, still, he paid little heed if his wives or women slaves conversed with me when we should meet outside in the greater court, or if I should en-counter them in the bazaar of the town. Indeed he would some-times send me trading to the 'dakakin' in company with his head wife and some of her women, in order that I might assist them in carrying home some of the things they bought.

And in this way I became acquainted with a woman slave of the name of Erega, belonging to the Marghi tribe. And there sprang up a love between us, and we sought many opportunities of meeting in secret, and this the head wife found out and told my master, who was exceedingly wroth, and vowed that he would punish me, and he had me tied to a stake and flogged on the back until I fainted; and to another stake the Marghi girl was also tied, and would have been flogged, but that she swore by God and the Earth that no harm had passed between us, and that the head wife had only accused her out of jealousy; and as she was a comely girl, and a favourite with the old Pul-o, he was inclined to believe her, and she was released; but he still said that on the morrow he would sell me to the Turks.

And all that night I remained tied by my wrists to the post where I had been flogged; but just before the dawn, when every

one was sleeping soundly, the young Marghi girl, who had managed to get out of the harim, came to my side with a knife and
cut my bonds, and then bade me run away, and hide until my
master's wrath had spent itself. This I needed no second bidding
to do, and, sore as I was with my beating, I crept cautiously to
the gateway of the courtyard, and putting aside the beam, and
opening the wooden door noiselessly, I fled into the town.

Before it was yet light I had hidden in one of the masajid
(mosques), and waited until daylight. Then I made for one of
the gates of the town, thinking to pass out into the country and
hide in the bush for awhile; but the soldiers who stood at the
gates would not let me pass, seeing me naked and my back all
bloody, and suspecting me to be a runaway slave.

When I told them what had happened to me, disguising such
of my tale as would make them think I had been justly punished, they took pity on me, and one of their number said he
would take me to the great Sultan of the town—the Amir of
Yakuba—and as I limped alongside of this soldier, who was on
horseback, my heart quaked within me, for I said to myself,
'Surely the Amir is a great man, and will know the truth, and
will return me to my master!' But I dared not run away from
the soldier, lest worse should befall me. And when the soldier
dismounted and led me into the Sultan's palace, I could not feel
my feet touch the ground, such was the fear and awe that possessed me. After a while life came back to me, and I lifted up
my eyes, and looked up at the Sultan when my companion
nudged me.

He was a tall Pul-o, with a yellow face marked with smallpox,
and with a thick black beard. Below his eyes was a thin blue
veil covering his nose, mouth, and chin, and falling over his
breast, so that when he spoke his voice sounded far away and
muffled.

The soldier told him my tale, and he listened attentively, and

then addressed me with somewhat of kindness, saying that he
would inquire further into the matter when he had leisure, and
telling the soldier to take me away, to wash my wounds, and
clothe me in a taub and a turban, and to give me food, and bring
me back towards eventide, when the Sultan should have returned from his prayers at the masjid.

At eventide, then, the Sultan saw me again, and this time
my heart was strengthened, for I was clothed in a fine new blue
taub and a clean white turban, and my belly was full with maize-
porridge, and I thought myself a fine fellow and a regular Muslim; and the Sultan made me tell him all my history, from the
time when I was captured by the Ful-be, and especially he asked
me many questions about my Pul-o master, old Nyebbu, inquir-
ing about his wealth, and how much ivory he had, and how
many slaves and guns, and asking me to tell him everything I
knew. And when I had answered as near as I could all these
questions, and seeing from his manner that the Sultan seemed
rather jealous of Nyebbu, a 'Shaitan'[45] put it into my heart to
tell lies that should hurt my master; and I told the Sultan I had
heard Nyebbu say many times that he was the greatest man in
Yakuba, and that when the right day came he would depose the
Amir and make himself Sultan in his stead, and that he had
sent a great present to the Amir-al-Mumenin at Sakatu to gain
his favour, so that he might win him over to his side.

And these latter words were not altogether a lie, for I had
seen my master despatch this present to Wurno, but with what
purpose I do not know. And after I had finished talking I could
see that the Sultan was in a mighty rage against my master, for
his eyes blazed, and by pulling at his veil with his hands he tore
it. When I had done talking he said nothing, but dismissed me,
and told me to return to the soldiers in the courtyard, who
would feed me and treat me well; but on no account was I to
leave his palace, or he would have me killed.

'The Sultan was sitting on his carpet smoking a water-pipe.'

The next day a messenger came to fetch me to the palace of
the Sultan of Yakuba, and when I arrived there and arose from
touching the ground with my forehead, I saw standing in the
corner of the diwan my Pul-o master, who had two guards on
either side of him, with drawn swords: his hands were tied together behind his back, and he looked in a sorry plight, with
his clothes torn, and his face bloody where some soldier had
struck him in arresting him.

When his eyes met mine, they lit up with wrath, but he said
nothing, and I, knowing myself to be in favour with the Sultan,
met his gaze proudly, arranged my new turban, and smoothed
down the folds of my new taub so that he might see I was now
in good circumstances. The Sultan was sitting on his carpet
smoking a water-pipe. His executioner, a tall Kanuri man with
a red fez, naked to the waist, and having a great red cloth round
his loins, stood by the Sultan's side with a drawn sword. When
I had remained there waiting for some few moments, the Sultan
removed the mouthpiece of the pipe from his lips and said:—

'Repeat now the charges thou didst bring yesterday against
thy master Nyebbu, and if thou shouldst have lied to me, and I
find it out, I shall know how to deal with thee.'

Then my heart waxed faint within me lest the Sultan should
of his wisdom discover the lies I had told, but I plucked up
courage, thinking that it was only my word against my master's,
and that the latter was jealously regarded by the Sultan, and I
resolved to tell the same tale as I had related the day before.

When I had finished, the Sultan turned to my master and
said:—'Thou hast heard the words of this slave, O Nyebbu!
What hast thou to say in thy defence?'

And my master replied, his voice shaking with anger, 'It is a
cunning mixture of truth and lies which the slave has told, O
Sultan! This and this is true, but that and that is false. It is true
that I have sent ivory to thy liege lord the Amir-al-Mumenin,

as a compliment, but it is less than the present I gave thee. It is false that the thought ever entered my heart, or the words ever passed my lips, that I wished to conspire against thy power or make myself Sultan in thy stead. It is true that I gave this dog a flogging; and I blame myself only that my heart was soft, and that, for the offence he committed, I did not have him killed outright. Now I take Allah to witness that I have not sinned in aught against my allegiance to thee and thy rule, and I pray thee, as a just man, and one fearing God, to release me from my bonds and hand over to me for punishment this lying slave. Thou hast the power to do me to death, I know, but assuredly Allah and the Amir-al-Mumenin, thy lord, will require my blood at thy hands.'

When he had ceased speaking, the Sultan rose in wrath, and called out to those of his guards and courtiers who were around him, 'Is not this man self-condemned? Do you not hear the proud fashion in which he talks? What care I for the Amir of Sakatu? Is he lord over me? I, the Sultan of Yakuba, of Bautshi, of Muri, of Soso?[46] It is enough: the slave has spoken truth. Strike off the head of Nyebbu, and we will see whether his friend, the Amir of Sakatu, can help him; and cut out the tongue of this dog, and son of a dog, in that he has dared to invoke the name of Allah to support his false statements.'

When my master heard these words, he shook himself free of his guards, and, throwing himself flat on his stomach, he managed, as best he could with his tied hands, to wriggle to the Sultan's feet, crying, 'Aman! Aman! O my lord! be merciful— spare my life, and let me live yet a little while, and I will be thy slave: I will be content to light thy pipe and boil the kettle for thy *tshai*. Take, take all that is mine—my ivory, and slaves, and women—if thou seest good; but let me yet live a little while. I will start on the Haj to Mekka. I will pray for thee there at the Holy places.'

And thus he wept, and groaned, and called aloud, and even turned his face towards me, saying, 'Speak thou in my favour, O Horejandu![47] I have ever treated thee kindly since the day I bought thee at Yola.' But I spurned his face with my foot, and said, 'Who am I that I should dare to speak when the Sultan has spoken?' And the Sultan called out in an angry voice, 'I am weary of this noise. Are you all, then, as this man, that you look to the Amir of Sakatu, and not to me—that I speak and you obey not?'

And the guards seized my master without more ado, and dragged him to the steps of the outer court. Here, while the Pul-o merchant was still calling out on his rough treatment, they thrust a wooden gag into his mouth, so that it pried his jaws open; and, when this was done, the executioner took from his waistband a pair of iron pincers, and, seizing my master's tongue, tore it out by the roots; and then, tying him against a wooden block in the centre of the courtyard, the executioner sliced off his head at one blow. And his head was stuck on a post outside the Sultan's gateway, and the body we dragged about the town by the legs, shouting out that thus should all people be treated that despised the authority of the Sultan of Yakuba; and the body was afterwards flung outside the town for the hyenas to eat. And, after Nyebbu had been executed, the Sultan sent men to seize all his property and slaves, and he attached me to his own household, and gave me the Marghi girl to wife, the same that belonged to my late master; and I became a great favourite with the Sultan of Yakuba, and was much feared in the town, for it was said, 'Whomsoever Horejandu condemns, him the Sultan executes.'

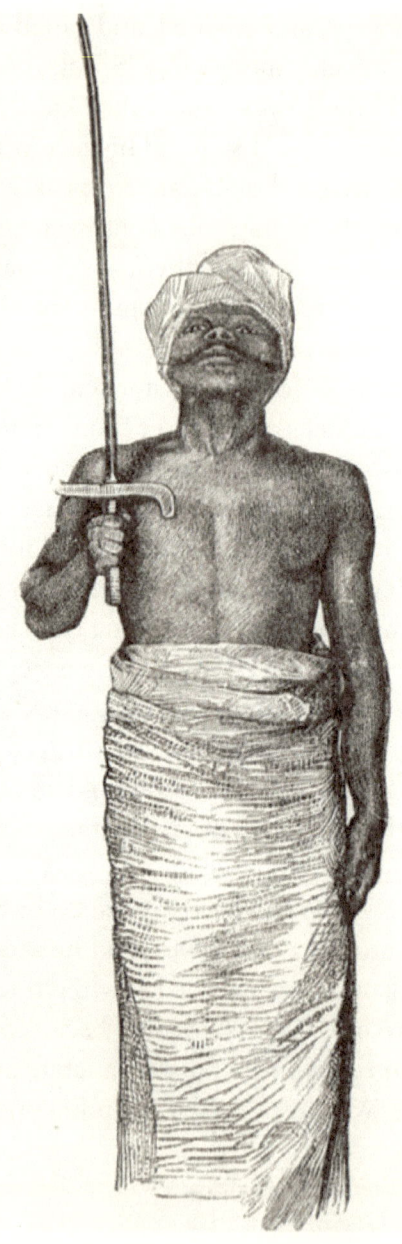

'His executioner, a tall Kanuri man with a red turban, naked to the waist,
stood by the Sultan's side with a drawn sword.'

'And his head was stuck on a post, and the body we dragged about the town by the legs.'

CHAPTER XI.

SO my affairs prospered for the space of a year or more, but, meanwhile, some Ful-be in the town, who liked not the Sultan of Yakuba, had sent secret messages to Wurno[48] to tell the Amir-al-Mumenin the things which Mohammed Sadiku,[49] the Sultan of Yakuba, had done, and the way in which he had repudiated his allegiance to his liege lord of Sakatu; and after some fourteen months had passed the rumour reached us that a great army was on its way from Kano to punish Sadiku, and set up another Sultan in his stead, who should govern Yakuba for the Amir of Sakatu.

And these things caused great terror to my new master, the Sultan, who sent messengers in all directions to all parts of his dominions to collect his fighting men and defend his capital; and the walls of the town were repaired and made good, much store of provisions were collected therein, and there was constant drilling of troops all day, and serving out of gunpowder, and lead to cast into bullets. And at length we could see from the great mountain behind Yakuba the smoke of burning villages, and other signs of the devastating army; and soon a great host was encompassing the town on all save the mountain side. And, seeing the great forces brought to subdue Yakuba, the Ful-be notables of the town held council among themselves in secret conclave, and they said to each other, 'Wherefore should we join issue with this man who has been Sultan of Yakuba? His quarrel is not our quarrel. Why should we fight to save him from the rule of the great Amir of Sakatu? We are Ful-be, and the Sultan of Sakatu is a Pul-o, and the Prince of the True Believers. Surely it would be a sin in Allah's eyes to fight against

him. Let us then send out messengers from the town to the commander of the host, and ask him for protection and a guarantee
of our property, if we come to terms with him, and hand over to
his keeping the man who has been Sultan here.'

And news was brought to me of what the Ful-be elders had
planned by one who was my friend in this council; and I went
in to my master, the Sultan, and told him secretly what was in
the wind. And he trembled much and turned ashy pale, and said
to me:

'I see clearly that the men of the town have no gratitude in
their hearts for what I have done for them, and will not stand
by me. When I call upon them to fight they will go over to the
enemy, even if they do not first surround my palace and capture
me, and give me over to my enemies as a prisoner. There is nothing for it therefore but to escape to the mountains while there is
yet time. Do thou therefore make ready for me food that I may
take away with me; and at nightfall I will disguise myself, and
bear an order, sealed with my own seal, that shall let me pass out
at the mountain gate, and so I will hide among the hill people
till I can find means to escape to the kingdom of Adamawa,
where I have friends; and as for thee, thou shalt go with me and
follow my fortunes, and, if thou art true to me, when Allah shall
again give me prosperity, I swear by Allah I will reward thee. I
will make thee a rich man and free. 'See,' he said, 'thou had
nought to gain by turning against me as those traitors have done,
and thou art more hated in the town perhaps than even I am,
and they would be sure to kill thee when I am gone.'

And this reflection was a true one, and seeing that I had nothing to gain by betraying my master, I resolved to escape from the
town with him, and follow him wheresoever he should go.

So we hastily and secretly set to work to make preparations
for the journey, and the Sultan filled a bag with silver riyalat
(dollars), which he hung round his neck, and he wrote out with

*'Stealthily walking through the streets of the town
where the shadows were deepest.'*

his own pen, on a piece of sheep-skin, an order to let himself and myself pass out of the gate, only he called us by the names of two of his servants; and he hid about his person such small things as he could hastily lay his hands on, and I did the same, also preparing some balls of cooked yam and maize cakes; and we put over all these things several rich taubs and scarves, and hid our faces with lishams or face-veils, such as the Ful-be of the North are given to wear, and arming ourselves secretly with daggers and loaded pistols—the Sultan carried a pistol with six barrels, such as you call 'riwolwa,' which had been sent him as a present by the Christian traders on the Kwara—we left the palace.

Stealthily walking through the streets of the town where the shadows were deepest, we arrived at the mountain-gate, and the Sultan speaking in a muffled voice showed his written pass to the captain of the guard, and told him to let us quickly pass on the Sultan's business. And the captain of the guard, suspecting nothing, touched the permit with his forehead in token of respect, and gave orders to his men that they should cautiously unbar the gates and let us through. So we passed out of the town and climbed up into the mountain, where we hid ourselves amongst the stones and bushes.

When the dawn came we could look out over the town, and, fearing to leave our place of hiding in daylight whilst so many scouts of the Kano army were scouring the plains, we resolved to lay quiet all that day until darkness should again set in, and we could venture to cross the open country at night. And soon after the sun was up we could see that there was a great commotion inside the town and out, for the leaders had evidently discovered our flight, and had sent to treat with the commander of the Sakatu army. When it was about mid-day the gates of the town were opened, and after much firing of guns the besieging force marched in.

What happened afterwards we did not know, for as no one was sent searching for us we cautiously crept down the other side of the mountain where there were no inhabitants, crawling cautiously among the stones and bushes, and keeping ever a good look-out that no one spied us. When the sun was setting we were at the base of the mountain, and there being a moon that night we made the best of our way on foot across the plain until we came to some hills, where we hid for awhile. And the next day we waded across the shallow part of a river, and bought a little food at a small village of Bautshi people, who wondered greatly to see us Mohammedans on foot, but we explained to them that our caravan had been broken up by the invading army, and our camels taken from us. And here, with three of the silver riyalat, we managed to buy two small asses, which we mounted, and then rode on as quickly as might be in a southerly direction, crossing a great plain between two ranges of mountains; and when we had been travelling thus for some three days we arrived at a quiet valley between some downs, where there were no people dwelling.

The punishment of Allah fell upon my master, the Sultan, here. We had made ourselves a small camp for the night by cutting down thorn-bushes and strewing them in a circle, and inside these we tethered our asses, and the Sultan lit a fire with his flint and steel and tinder, and when we had eaten, and washed our hands with sand, and prayed, the Sultan laid down to sleep, and bade me watch until it was the middle of the night, when I should sleep, and he would take his turn of watching.

But after awhile it was fated that my eyelids should grow heavy, and slumber fall upon me, so that I ceased to watch; and when I had slept for a little while I was awakened by the firing of a pistol, and then I heard the growling of a lion and the voice of my master calling for help. And it would seem that whilst I slept the fire had gone out, and a hungry lion had leapt the barrier of thorns, and fastened on to one of the asses, who in terror broke loose from the stake to which it was tethered, and struck my master with its hoofs as he slept, and he, starting up in a fright, and seeing by the light of the waning moon that a lion was attacking the ass, pulled out his 'riwolwa' and fired it at the body of the lion, at the same time calling on me to help him; and the lion, being wounded in the back and greatly enraged, left the ass which he was tearing and fell on my master, whose arm and leg he tore with his teeth and claws; but my master, fighting for his life, fired off all the other barrels of the 'riwolwa' into the lion's head with the other hand, which was free, and the lion left off biting him and fell dead.

Then I, who had scarce known whether I was alive or dead with the fright I had had, arose, and seeing the lion was dead, I dragged his body from off my master, whom I also took for dead, but he had only fainted from loss of blood.

I got the flint and steel from his waist-cloth and struck a light, and having made a blaze of dried twigs, I tore off long strips of cloth from my master's clothes, and bound up the great wounds in his thigh and arm where the lion had torn him.

And when it was morning I saw my master had opened his eyes and was looking round, but a fever had got hold of him, and he talked nonsense, and he knew not where he was nor what had happened to him. I tended to his wants as well as I could, and then, bethinking myself that he was too ill to continue his journey then, and that the ass which the lion had attacked was also in a sorry condition, I thought it best to remain where we were till my master should have recovered; and so I took our two gourds and went out to seek water, that I might have wherewith to quench our thirst and wash my master's wounds.

And when I had ascended a little hillock, where there was rain-water lying in the clefts of the rocks, I spied in the distance, riding slowly across the plain, some Ful-be horsemen. Guessing that they were on the look-out for my master, I hurried back to our encampment, which was on the other side and shielded from their sight. Then I stamped out the fire, so that its smoke should not betray the whereabouts of the camp to the Ful-be, and sat down to reflect on what I should do; and, seeing that my master lay sick and out of his senses, and that one of the asses, too, was disabled, I resolved within myself that it was foolish to remain with my master any longer, for it would be long ere he could travel, and then only slowly, and assuredly the Ful-be would discover us and slay us. So, having considered all this, I went to my master, who was talking nonsense and heeded me not, and took from his neck the bag of dollars which he carried, and the 'riwolwa,' and whatever other things of value were easy to stow away; and then, leaving him a gourd of water, a little food, and the disabled ass, I mounted the other and rode away towards the high range of hills in the west, knowing the hillock where I had been to get the water would for some time screen me from the gaze of the Ful-be horsemen; and at nightfall I reached a village at the base of the mountains.

Here I gave myself out to be a Hausa trader, for the people were foolish, timid pagans, who, seeing me dressed like a Hausa, believed me to be such.

I had not any clear plan in my mind as to what course I should pursue; but I, in my ignorance of the purposes of Allah, thought I was now far enough away from pursuit, and would give myself out as a free man, and could trade with the dollars I had taken from my master. So I told all the villagers that I was riding in front of a large caravan of slaves from the Adamawa countries, and wished to know where in that direction I should find a great market at which I could profitably dispose of my slaves. And they, in their foolishness, said, 'Why not go to Yakuba? There is no better place to sell slaves than in Yakuba.'

'A hungry lion had leapt the barrier of thorns, and fastened on to one of the asses, who in terror broke loose from the stake to which it was tethered.'

But I told them I had heard there was a glut of slaves in that market, and asked if they knew of no great town to the westward. On that they counselled me to proceed to Keffi, which should be a town nearly as big as Yakuba, lying to the westward. And they directed me to proceed along a certain little river to a place where it joined a bigger stream, and after crossing at the ford, skirting a great mountain, and crossing another river, I should then see Keffi before me. And believing in the tale that I told them, they asked me before leaving to give them some guarantee that my big caravan, which they supposed to be following me, should not harass them as it passed through their town, and I, wishing to satisfy them and get free, pulled out the pass which the Sultan of Yakuba had written, and gave it into their hands, they, of course, not being able to read what was thereon written.

And then by the earliest morning I rode off in the direction of Keffi. And after several days' journey, which would be wearisome to recount to you, I found myself at the gates of this great town, and had to sleep outside all the night, because I arrived after sundown, and the gates were shut; and I was much harassed by the attacks of the hyenas, who would run in on me and snap at my own limbs or the legs of my ass.

CHAPTER XII.

WHEN I entered Keffi the next morning I was an over-confi-
dent fool, believing that the townspeople of that place would
as readily believe my lies as the simple villagers in the wilder-
ness. So in the market-place I told all who questioned me that
I was a Hausa merchant come to trade there, to buy slaves with
riyalat; and I said how the rest of my caravan had been broken
up and dispersed by the attacks of robbers, and I only had escaped. And hearing this story several traders came forward and
spoke to me in the Hausa language. I stammered and stuttered.
I could not speak that tongue, and replied to them in the Ful
speech, and they laughed aloud at me, and cried out, 'What are
these lies thou tellest us? Thou a Hausa merchant, and canst
not speak the Hausa tongue? And the Fulful-de thou talkest is
the Fulful-de of a slave. Perchance thou art some runaway that
hath robbed his master and donned his clothes. Come along
with us to the governor of the town, and give us a true state-
ment of thy case.'

And though I protested, and swore, and entreated, and several times wrenched my garments from their grasp, they dragged
me from off the ass and led me to the Hausa governor of that
town, which although in the empire of the Amir of Sakatu is
ruled by Hausas; and when I was carried before the governor,
so great was my fear that my wit deserted me and I could not
frame a lie that should satisfy them, but blurted out the whole
truth of what had befallen me before I came to Yakuba; and I
was long in the telling of the tale, but encouraged to proceed,
and cheered in the telling by the laughter of the governor, who
made merry over the things I had done. When I had finished

119

speaking he bade them strip me of all my clothes and dollars, and everything I possessed, so that I was stark naked.

'Now,' he said, 'thou deservest death for the things thou hast done; but I have not the heart to kill thee, for thou hast made my sides ache with laughter. Thou shalt live, therefore, and become my slave. But beware lest thou play any pranks with me. I have more wisdom than Nyebbu and Sadiku.'

So he bade his servants give me an old piece of cloth to hide my nakedness, and sent me to work in his plantations.

This was a bitter lot for me, who had thought myself almost a Mohammedan gentleman; and often I would stop to weep at the misfortunes that had befallen me. And thus, when I failed to do good work, I got many a flogging from the overseer of the governor's plantation; and one day it was said to me that as I was a worthless slave I should be sold in the market.

So, together with some others, who were wild bushmen from the Akpoto[50] country, that had been captured in a Hausa raid across the Benue, we were taken on a great fair day to the town of Keffi, and stationed there in the market-place for sale. And a Hausa merchant of Kano looked at me, examined me, and asked many questions about me, and, finally, after much talking with the overseer, bought me for fourteen dollars: and two days afterwards my new master set out for Kano, with a big caravan, with many camels and horses and asses and slaves; and my neck was set in a great wooden collar, the other end of which was fastened to the neck of another slave; and thus, with pain and weariness, we had to walk on day after day in the middle of the caravan; and although I pleaded many times to be set free to walk by myself, and swore every oath I could think of not to run away, the leader of the caravan had no pity on me, and said he had heard in Keffi I was a cunning rascal, and he did not intend to give me any chance of escape.

I do not know how I lived through this journey, so great was

'Often I would stop to weep at the misfortunes that had befallen me.'

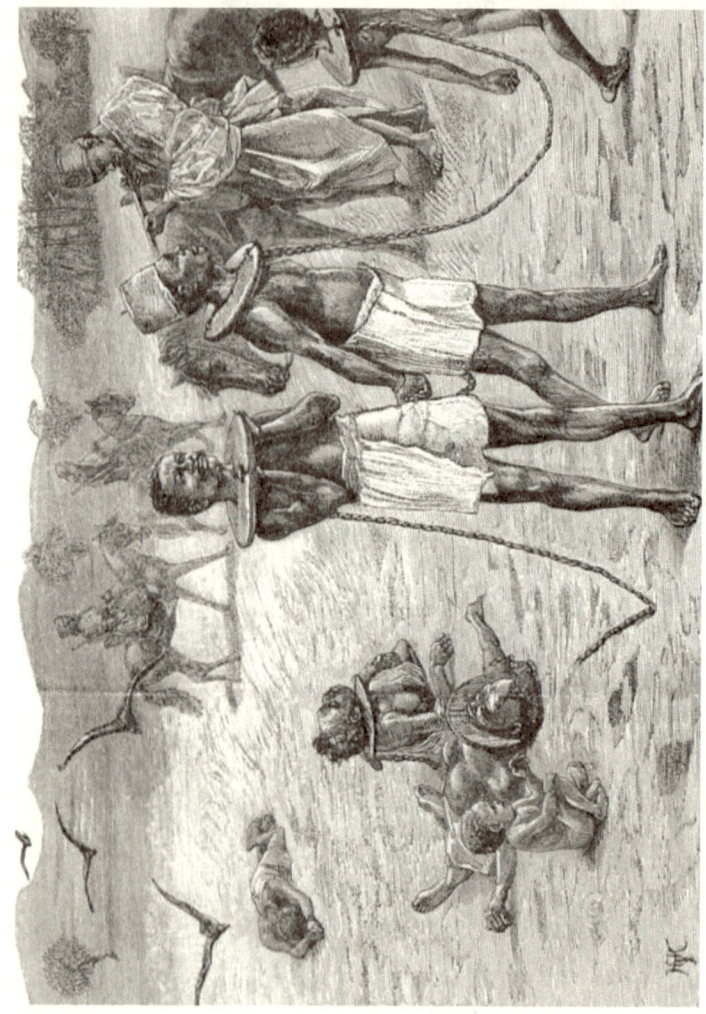

'I was now forced to walk in step with a poor wild pagan slave from the Ibo country, joined to him during the march by a chain which united our heavy wooden collars.'

my suffering and so little had I to eat. The great wooden collar that I wore round my neck was never removed, and its chafing caused two great sores to come on my shoulders, the scars of which I bear to this day. The Hausa man, who was the 'Maid-oki,'[51] or leader of the caravan, was called Shekara.[52] He was a cruel man with a hard heart, and paid no heed to my whining nor yet to my compliments, for at first I thought to win his favour by extolling his greatness or the beauty of his countenance or the splendour of his horse-trappings as he rode past us, but he would only aim a blow at my head with the butt of the lance that he carried, and rebuke me for a saucy slave in daring to comment on a person of his greatness.

I, who had been a favourite of the Sultan of Yakuba, and considered myself as much a Muslim as any Arab or Pul-o follower of the Prophet, I was now forced to walk in step with a poor wild pagan slave from the Ibo country, joined to him during the march by a chain which united our heavy wooden collars. Sometimes I would try to show the guards of the caravan that I was a Muslim like themselves, and in a loud voice I would recite the Fatha, the prayer from the Book of books which I had picked up from the Ful-be Muslemin, or I would attempt to pray the Two-Bow Prayer,[53] but so often as I did this in the hearing of the guards they would strike me on the mouth and jeer at me, saying that Allah could not understand such jargon, and mocking me for the nonsense that I spoke in the Arabic I had learnt by rote.

We sojourned for awhile at a place called Saria,[54] and here the slave to whom I was fastened fell sick and died, and a number of other slaves of the caravan also perished, so much so that the leader feared to lose all his profits; so he consulted with some of his men, and it was agreed that such of us as had survived the sickness should be somewhat better treated, so that we might reach Kano in fair condition. Moreover, the wooden collar was taken from my neck, and the sores were dressed with oil, and a large rope was tied round my throat instead, and this in turn fastened to another slave. I was given a little more food than before, and our progress was slower between Saria and Kano, so that the slaves might not become too exhausted.

At length one day the soldiers in front of the caravan began firing their guns and shouting, and the word passed along that Kano was in sight.

This was a finer city than any I had yet seen, and although I was sick and weak, and an ill-treated slave, even I felt glad, and walked in a more upright manner as I passed through the great gate and entered the streets of the town. We slaves were all taken to the slave market to be sold next day, but this did not make us sad in any way, for we felt that, whatever our lot might be, it could not be worse than our previous sufferings, and we were even merry as we sat over a huge dish of porridge that night.

The next morning there was a great press of people in the market, where each lot of slaves with their sellers were stood in a row for purchasers to inspect. There were Arabs, Kanuri people from Bornu, Tawarek[55] from the Great Desert, and Ful-be from Sakatu and the Kwara River, all wishing to purchase slaves. A Hausa man of Kano, whose name was Gungi, and who was a 'Mairini,'[56] or dyer, examined me very closely, and asked many questions about me. Of course the Hausa who bought me in Keffi spoke highly of my qualities, and said there never was such a strong and willing worker as I, but the dyer looked doubtfully at me, because of my great leanness and the sores on my body. However, at last, after much dispute he bought me for thirty thousand kurdi[57] (kauri shells), and took me away with him to his house, which was in the quarter of the town called Sherbale.[58]

When we were arrived he spoke to me in Fulful-de, which I

In the slave market.

then knew better than Hausa, and told me that if I was a good slave I should find in him a kind master, but that if I shirked my work, or stole, or ran away, I should find no pity in his heart. I spoke many sweet things to him, and knelt to him, and kissed his hand, and won his favour, for he looked kindly on me. Then he clapped his hands, and when some women slaves came he bade them lead me to a small tank of water, where I could wash, and afterwards to give me food. He also sent a small boy to me whilst I was washing, with a common blue taub of cotton and an old red fez, and told me to wear these instead of the dirty rags I wore about my body. Having washed and put on my new clothes, I looked quite a better kind of man, and my new master—Baba Gungi, as he was called —took great credit to himself for having made such a cheap bargain in the market.

In the afternoon of that day Baba Gungi took me with him to his 'Marina,' at the back of his yard. This was an open terrace or platform of clay, with a number of clay dyeing-pots, and three slaves were here stirring up the indigo juice that was in the pots, and mixing it every now and then with some pounded red wood, of a kind brought from Adamawa.

My master spoke to these other slaves, and told them to instruct me in the work and make me useful. When he had left us, his slaves, who were rather simple folk, and mostly people from Bornu, asked me to tell them something of myself—who I was and whence I came, and to them I related much of my past adventures as I have told them to you, and in this way we sat long talking until they heard the sound of our master's sandals pattering on the ground of the courtyard outside, and started up in a panic to go back to their work.

Then I was shown by one of them how I must fetch a white cotton taub from among a bundle that lay on a clay bench that ran along one side of the marina, and soak it in a tank of clean water; and when this was done wring it out nearly dry, and then

Beating the taubs.

plunge it into one of the dye-pots, where another man stirred
it round with a stick. And then, again, I was to take other shirts
from the other dye-pots, the dyeing of which was finished, and,
having wrung them out, to plunge them for a minute into another tank of dirty water, and then again wringing them out, to
hang them on the branch of a small tree which grew in the middle of the dyeing-place; and, when this was done, and whilst
these shirts were set to dry, I was given others that were already
dried, and these I had to spread out on mats on the ground of
the marina, and beat first one side and then the other with a
long, pliant stick. This was a business hard to learn, for the
taubs must be beaten in a certain fashion, so that the roughness
of the dye leaves the cotton, and a shiny appearance, like silk,
takes its place. All through the day we would hear this sound
of beating the taubs going on, for always one slave or another
was at the work; and, as they beat, they would sing this song in
unison with the sound of the blows:

Mu Masurini ne!
Dafari mu-rina riga,
Baya ga mu-buga riga,
Anshima mu-tala ta
Ga mutum kiau![59]

We are dyers!
First we dye the shirt,
Then we beat the shirt,
And then we sell it
To a goodly man

For the first few weeks that I lived in Kano I sought only to
gain the favour of my master, and I was so industrious in this
dyeing work that the other slaves reported well of me to Baba

Gungi. But after a time I wearied of this life, although I had plenty to eat and a master who did not ill-treat me. I began in time to assume a mastery over the other slaves of the marina, and became a kind of chief among them—so much so that I made them do all the work, and passed my time mostly joking and laughing with my master's women.

And occasionally I would manage to have a little dyeing done privately for such friends as I had made in the town, and for this they would give me small presents, so that I could gradually store up money with which to buy fine clothes. And my master at first approved of my smart appearance, and told me that I did credit to his household; but gradually he grew distrustful, and suspected that I had not dealt quite honestly with him; moreover, he grew angry at my behaviour with the women, and at the saucy tone I took when he rebuked me, and I heard him say one day to another of the slaves that he would find means to reduce my pride.

One morning he found great fault with the dyeing of some taubs, and ordered me to repeat the process. I called another of the slaves, and bid him dip the taubs again into the dyeing-pots, but my master angrily interrupted and said: 'I ordered thee to do it, thou dog, and not Brahimu. It is time thou shouldst be punished for thy insolence.' And he stepped into the house, and fetched thence a great whip made of hippopotamus hide.

I was standing with my back to him, mocking his wrath to the other slaves, when he suddenly began to lash me with this whip, and even through the cotton shirt which covered my shoulders he cut my flesh with the whip and drew blood. I could not contain myself at this treatment, so I turned on him with all my strength—for I am a strong man, which is why the Arabs call me Abu-l-guwah—and, lowering my head, I charged at him like a bull, butting him full in the stomach. Such was the force of my blow that the whip fell from his hand, and he sank to the

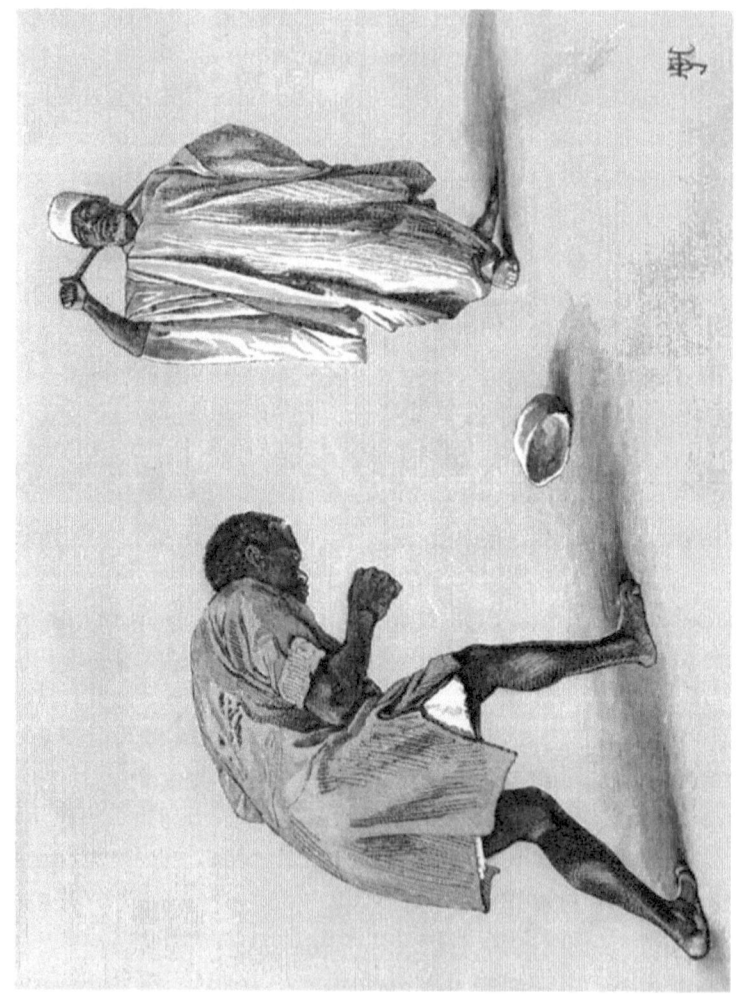

'Lowering my head, I charged at him like a bull, butting him full in the stomach.'

ground like a dying man.

When the other slaves saw that I had seemingly killed their master they raised a terrible noise, and all the women came into the marina shrieking and tearing their garments and calling for help. Remembering what had happened to me at Yakuba, before any could detain me I broke from them all, and ran full pelt through the streets to the palace of the Ghaladima,[60] or governor of the town, and heeding not the clamour of the guards, I rushed on blindly into the diwan, where the governor was sitting on his carpet. Seizing the skirt of his long robe in one hand, I cried 'Aman! Aman! I place myself under thy protection.' And he proudly removed his garment from my hand, called to his guards to seize me, and demanded to know why I had been allowed to enter his presence. And they, bowing their foreheads to the dust, protested humbly that I must be a madman, a possessed, that there was no holding me, that I passed through them like one of the Jann.[61] And then the Sultan demanded of me to tell him my tale; and I related to him so much of my history as might bear on the case, laying great stress on the fact that I was a Muslim, and had been a big chief in my own country, and that to be struck by another man put madness in my heart. And the Sultan said to me: 'Knowest thou how to fight, how to aim with a gun, how to ride a horse in battle?' And I replied that I had been a great warrior in my own land, and had slain many people.

Then he asked me if I were willing to become one of his soldiers; and I said: 'Ay, Wallah, if thou grant me protection!' Then he handed me over to the 'Sarki-n-yaki,'[62] the captain of the guard, that he should drill me as a soldier.

Once more my heart felt proud at the change in my fortunes, and the other soldiers amongst whom I now lived treated me with a certain amount of respect, as being a slave who had killed his master and yet had got off scathless. It took me some time to learn to ride a horse in the same fearless fashion as the other troopers rode; but I had lost my fear of that animal, and the horses of Hausa-land are smaller and more docile than those of the Arabs in Tarabulus. We were armed with a straight sword, which was hung on our left side, and in the right hand we carried a long heavy spear. The officers of the troop wore daggers, fastened in a belt round their left arm; and a few of us had muskets, which we carried in place of the spear, and those who had muskets—I was one—daily practised firing at a target. We wore red fezzes on our heads, and we dressed in large blue shirts round the breast and down to the hips; these were bound close to the body by means of a red shawl, which we wound tightly about us. Some of the officers had their black shawls tied over the lower part of their faces, after the fashion of the Tawarek. We wore no sandals on our feet, because they interfered with our grasp of the stirrups. This cavalry, which was in the service of the Sultan of Kano, was quartered in barracks at the back of the palace, and these barracks enclosed a square, or maidan, where we could drill or exercise with our horses.

About what happened further, when I went to war for the Sultan of Kano, I will tell you when I see you to-morrow. *Insh-allah, ma tashuf ash-shurr!*

CHAPTER XIII.

WHEN I had served in the army of the Sultan of Kano for perhaps six months, we were ordered to get ready to go on a warlike expedition. The Sarki[63]—as the Hausa people called their Sultan—the Sarki of Kano had arranged a very clever plan. Some little while before the Sultan of Gujeba,[64] a town in the Bornu territories, had sent an invitation to him to join in a raid on the pagans of Kalam;[65] but the Kano Sultan excused himself by saying that he had other concerns in which he wished to employ his army. Nevertheless he urged the Sultan of Gujeba to exterminate in Kalam all such as should not have embraced the true faith; and, as soon as he satisfied himself that the Sultan of Gujeba had set out on his expedition with all his forces, and that the frontier lands of Bornu were denuded of soldiers, he gave orders to the commander of his army, Sheik Abd-er-Rahman (a Moor, who had risen to a high position in the service of the Sultan of Kano), to get ready four thousand cavalry and about twenty thousand foot soldiers, armed with bows and spears and muskets, and invade the country of Katagum[66] and the border-lands of Bornu. Before the army left Kano many of us wished for charms against death, and several old 'figis' or 'm'alams' came, with their calabash inkstands and reed-pens, and wrote out verses from the Quran on sheep-skin.

When we left Kano we rode for about the space of half a day, and then stopped to encamp for the night, and the villagers of the district opened a market in our camp and sold provisions. At nightfall the leader of the camp sent for such of us as he esteemed for our valour, and gave us kola-nuts[67] to eat. We started again at midnight, when the waning moon was risen, and then

133

The Kano Cavalry.

made a long journey, even to the next evening. The day after that we arrived in the vicinity of a town called Gubu,[68] which our commander proposed to attack, as it was well populated. All the inhabitants round, at our approach, had flocked into Gubu, and defended themselves behind its walls, and also concealed themselves in the palm-groves and the stubble of the durrha-corn in its environs. They shot poisoned arrows and hurled darts at us: but we soon dislodged them from the vicinity of the town by setting fire to the stubble and such of the dry trees as would burn, and the raging of this fire swept the ground clean, and drove all the people into the town; and the next day we delivered the assault with the whole force, and easily carried the town by storm.

But the leader of our army, Abd-er-Rahman, was angry at the resistance they had made, and he cut off the heads of eight hundred of the defenders; and, having selected about two thousand of the best among the slaves, he despatched them with a small convoy back to Kano, whilst we proceeded further towards Katagum, leaving the town of Gubu not quite empty of inhabitants; for, as our commander said, we must allow some to remain behind to breed more slaves. The country of Katagum we utterly wasted and laid bare, and carried off a rich spoil of slaves, cattle, and camels; and after raiding as far as Fititi,[69] we reassembled our forces and returned to Kano.

I had agreed with some of my comrades that we should mutually assist each other in capturing slaves, and share the profits between us. The custom in that country is that, when a private soldier shall have caught, say, five slaves, he shall give two of them to the Sarki of Kano and retain the other three for himself—out of every five he must give up two to the governor. We—that is to say, my five comrades and myself—managed altogether to capture forty slaves, whom we bound one to the other and drove back before us when we were returning to Kano with the rest of the force. Of these forty some were old women, some were young girls and boys, and three or four were able-bodied men. We gave up sixteen of the slaves to the Sultan, taking care to choose the oldest and least valuable among them, and of the twenty-four that remained we each got four. Altogether, the whole amount of slaves collected with this raid numbered several thousand, and brought much wealth to the Sultan. At that time there was not a good market for slaves in Kano—there was no demand for them now by the merchants from the Kwara; so the Sultan of Kano resolved to send a strong slave caravan to Zinder,[70] a town about eight days' journey north of Kano; and he chose me as one of the escort, at which I greatly rejoiced, for I counted on selling at a good price my own four slaves. At the same time we had to convey presents and a letter to the Sarki of Zinder, who had recently allied himself to Kano against the Bornu people.

The commander of this expedition to Zinder—the 'Sarki-n-bai,'[71] or the 'Maidaria,'[72] as we used to call him—was a very jolly, good-tempered man, named Ubanmasifa. He was fond of jesting, and would often make us laugh loudly at his tales. He had taken a liking to me when we went on the slave raid to Katagum, and on this journey to Zinder he made me his Zaka-fada.[73] Several Moorish merchants from Fezzan accompanied us from Kano to Zinder, and with one of these—a man named Al-Haj-Ayub—I became very friendly, and he talked much to me of the fine things which were to be seen in his country, and in the land of the Turks at Tarabulus, and advised me to secretly leave the service of the Sarki of Kano, and accompany him on his return to Murzuk, whither he was going with a convoy of slaves and camels, for, he told me, camels were so cheap in Zinder that many people came across the Great Desert to buy them and take them back to Fezzan to sell again.

'We carried off a rich spoil of slaves, cattle, and camels.'

CHAPTER XIV.

IN our caravan, besides slaves, we carried a store of sweet pota-
toes and dried fish, which are things that may be profitably sold
in Zinder, where the people are far off from any big water that
holds fish, and for some reason or other cannot grow sweet po-
tatoes in their plantations. The road from Kano to Zinder is un-
safe travelling for small caravans, because of the robbers that
lurk in the woods, and some of these are Daura[74] people, who
are pagans and very fierce, and are constantly at war with the
people of both Zinder and Kano. They would lie in wait to attack even us, and would endeavour to surround and kill any
stragglers of the caravan, shooting poisoned arrows. The force
of their bows is so great that it is said their arrows will pierce
three planks of wood placed together, and the poison of them,
which is obtained from a certain plant, causes you to quickly
swell up and die, even if your skin is only just pricked with the
point of the arrow. We lost in this way one or two soldiers who
had lagged behind.

And another danger in this country was the many lions and
hyenas of a large kind, spotted, and not striped such as those
you see in Tarabulus. We had to make big fires at night-time to
keep off these beasts, and even then we were not safe, for one
night a lion and lioness jumped into our camp over the hedge
of thorns in a place where the fire had sunk low, and attacked
some of our horses, but we drove them off with burning brands.
The hyenas, however, as we neared Zinder, got so bold that they
would surround the camp at night in large numbers, and any
man who should venture outside alone would be attacked and
pulled down; and they had a cunning method of leaping at the

throats of such as they found alone and unprotected; and by seizing the necks of these people suddenly in their jaws, they would prevent their crying out.

After being about ten days on this route, we came within sight of Zinder, which we first discovered by the numbers of vultures that were circling round it in the air, for this great town lies a little low, and is concealed by a lot of rocks and low green hills. As soon as we entered the town, we of the escort who were taking the letter and the present from the Sarki of Kano to the Sarki of Zinder, went first to the house of the Ghaladima, the Wazir of the Sultan, and he, bidding us wait awhile in his outer court, hurried off to acquaint the Sarki of our coming, and arrange for an audience. The houses of Zinder seemed to us poor and dirty after those of Kano. The walls are simply of clay, baked in the sun, which has not been whitewashed nor decorated after the fashion of the Arabs. There is scarcely any furniture, and no mats or carpets to sit on; indeed, the Ghaladima himself was sitting in the dust.

After we had waited a short space of time, the Wazir returned and said the Sultan was ready to receive us, and, acting himself as a guide, he led us through the streets of the town to the Sultan's palace, which was a kind of mud fort. Herein we entered, and after passing through several courts where there were a lot of soldiers lounging about, all unarmed and bare-headed, clad in very dirty taubs, we were ushered into a dark chamber, where the Sultan was sitting on a mud bench. Instructed by the Wazir, we all threw ourselves down, and, taking up the dust of the floor in our hands, we threw it over our heads, saying in Hausa, 'Baba-n-sarki, Baba-n-sarki; Sarki-n-dunia!'[75]

Then, the Sultan having commanded us to deliver our message, we rose up and told him the occasion of our visit, and delivered to him the letter and the present which the Sarki of Kano had sent to him.

'One night a lion and lioness jumped into our camp . . . but we drove them off with burning brands.'

The Sultan ordered his people to fetch an old figi—an Arab from Wadai, who acted as his scribe —and when this man arrived he handed him the letter to read. Its contents pleased the Sultan, and he said that, in future, he should trust to Allah and the Sarki of Kano for the maintenance of his power, and not any longer to the Sheikh of Bornu, who had no business in his country, for in Zinder did they not speak Hausa and not Kanuri? And then he bade the Wazir give us each a present of kauri shells from the treasury, and supply us with food during our stay; and he told us that he would consider what reply he should send to the Sarki of Kano, and would give us a letter and a present to our Sultan when we should be ready to return to Kano.

After this we went out into the town, and visited such people as were persons of importance, paying many compliments, and receiving small presents in return. The next day we went to look at the slave-market to hear what prices were being given for slaves, but we found, to our disappointment, that they were of no more value here than at Kano, for the Sarki of Zinder had made many Ghazias[76] of late into the Daura country, and Zinder was full of slaves for sale. As I did not see any chance of getting a good price at present for my four slaves, whom I had brought with me, I resolved not to be in a hurry to sell them, although I had to feed them all this time.

The Sarki of Zinder is a cruel man, and much feared by his subjects and by the Tawarek of the desert who come to Zinder to trade. For the least offence he sentences people to death. When a criminal is to be killed he is taken by the executioner to an open place, underneath a lofty tree, with thick shiny leaves, of a kind called 'Alleluba' in the Hausa tongue. Of this sort of tree there are three or four only in Zinder, and each one is called 'Itatshe-n-mutua,'[77] which means the 'Tree of Death,' for these trees mark the places of execution upon the outskirts of the town.

A few days after we had come to Zinder we heard that a number of men, who had been caught stealing in the Sultan's plantations, were to be killed, and the Ghaladima sent a small boy to guide us to the place of execution, so that we might see how such things were carried on in Zinder.

We came, then, to one of these trees standing in an open space, which was bounded by great rocks, wherein the hyenas had their dens, and could eat the bodies of the people executed. The place under the shade of the tree was so clean swept and smooth that I went thither to seat myself out of the sun, but the boy who had come with us hastily snatched me back, and asked me if I wished to die.

'For,' he said, 'all such as go under the boughs of that tree, save the executioner, must die; and it is fortunate the executioner is not already here, or certainly thou wouldst have been hung up by the heels.'

When I heard these words I took care to get a safe distance from this Tree of Death, and I then observed that its upper branches were covered with innumerable vultures, who seemed to know, from the crowd of people standing under the place, that an execution had been ordered.

Presently the men doomed to death by the Sultan arrived, and fear was struck into all our hearts when we saw the manner of punishment ordered, and we wondered not the Sultan of Zinder had made himself greatly feared by his people.

There were six men this time to be killed. Their arms were bound to their sides and their ankles hobbled. Three of them the executioner tied round the neck and the ankles to the trunk of the tree, and then taking his long and straight sword he drove it into their bowels, and ripped them right up to the breastbone, after which he plunged in his hands and tore out their hearts, which he cast out to the vultures, who were thronging round him waiting for the offering.

The Tree of Death.

As to the other three, he first tied a rope round their ankles, and then seizing them as a man would seize a man in wrestling, turned them round on end on their heads, and while his assistant held them in this position, he threw the end of the rope over the lower branches of the tree, and then hung the man up by his heels. After hanging thus for a short while, the blood gushed from their mouths and nostrils, and in much agony they died.

But the last of these men, when the executioner was wrestling with him, bit him several times in the arms, so that he took out pieces of flesh with his teeth, and this so enraged the executioner that he changed the mode of punishment.

With the help of his attendants, he drew the rope through the man's armpits and then slung him up to the tree, so that his feet were a few inches from the ground. And when he was thus hung up perpendicularly, and swinging to and fro and turning round, the executioner took his sharp sword, and slowly cut the man to bits in little pieces, first lopping off the toes and then the fingers and the nose, and then slices from his arms and thighs, and every now and then he turned and made a jest to the people, who roared with laughter and clapped their hands in applause, after the Zinder fashion, and all the while the man who was being killed was screaming till my ears were deafened, and the vultures were nearly tripping up the executioner in their eagerness to snatch at the morsels that he hacked from the man.

At last the man had bled to death, and the executioner had cut off everything below his middle, and left the upper half of him still hanging to the tree. The people shrieked and applauded, and said there never was such an executioner in any town like theirs. But for my part I thought this a bad people, and surely such pastimes must be displeasing to Allah.

'The executioner every now and then turned and made a jest to the people.'

الْحَاج أَيُّوبَ مُرْزُكِي

Al-Haj-Ayub.

CHAPTER XV.

WE had been in Zinder some three weeks, and still the Sultan had not got ready his letter and his gift for Kano, and there seemed no chance of selling our slaves profitably. And I liked not this place, and ever felt fearsome and uneasy, for its people were insolent; and some who had seen me walk under the Tree of Death would tease me, and tell me that by rights I too should be executed.

This being so, I listened not unwillingly to my Fezzani friend, who proposed that I should join his caravan, and cross the Great Desert with him, assuring me that I should sell my slaves at great advantage at Murzuk, where the price is nearly ten times that of Zinder. Moreover, I might afterwards journey to the Turks' country on the sea coast, where I should see the wonders of the 'Nasrani,' and the great water, and the ships, and other things, the like of which I had never seen before.

The Fezzani, Al-Haj-Ayub, was a wise man, who had travelled far, and had been in Mekka, and even in the Balad-al-Hind,[78] and he told me privately the land of the blacks was 'batal'—worthless—and not to be named beside the lands of the Arabs and the Hindis, where the great Engrizi[79] ruled. So he advised me to secretly make all ready for my departure without arousing the suspicion of the leader of our expedition, the Sarki-n-bai; and then, when he sent me word to join him, to slip away from Zinder at night, and travel with the Airi[80] caravan, that he himself would accompany as far as the country of Azben; and to render this easier, he suggested that I should make a feint of selling to him the four slaves I possessed, and should also make over to him the camel I was to buy with the dollars and kauris I had hoarded in Kano and brought with me to Zinder; thus he could join my possessions to his own and take them out of Zinder in the caravan without arousing suspicion, and after I was well out of danger, on the road to Azben, he could return to me my own. This seemed to me a good plan, and I did as he directed, pretending to the Sarki-n-bai that I was tired of keeping the slaves, and had got a good price from Al-Haj-Ayub.

When the Airi caravan was ready to start—it was principally composed of Fezzani merchants and Ghadamsi traders returning across the desert with their slaves, and was escorted by Tawarek, who were paid to guard it safely as far as Agades—I received a secret message from Al-Haj-Ayub, telling me to leave Zinder at nightfall without arousing suspicion, and ride out to a small village under the hills to the north of the town, where I could join the caravan, which would halt there for the night. Accordingly I saddled my horse in the afternoon, and asking permission of the Sarki-n-bai to ride to the other end of the town and pay a visit to one of our friends, at whose plantation I said I would pass the night, I started, and when once outside the town rode rapidly to the village where I had appointed to meet Al-Haj-Ayub.

He arrived with the caravan soon after me, and paid me many compliments on my dexterity, telling me that I might rise to be a great man some day in the land of the Turks. I proposed that he should now restore me my camel and my four slaves, to one of whom, who was a girl from the town of Katagum, I had become much attached, and had resolved not to sell her. But Al-Haj-Ayub advised me in my own interest not to press such a request, for, he said, 'I have told the leader of the caravan that these slaves and this camel are mine, and that thou art my friend, who will accompany me as far as Azben on business for the Sarki of Kano, so it will be better not to alter this arrangement till we arrive at Azben; otherwise, knowing that thou wert a slave belonging to Kano, they might send thee back to the Sarki-n-bai at Zinder.'

This advice seemed reasonable, so I held my peace, though I was rather vexed that my woman-slave was placed with the women that accompanied Al-Haj-Ayub; but my Fezzani friend so talked me over that I resolved not to make any fuss until we were well beyond the limits of the Zinder territory. In this manner, appearing as the friend and companion of Al-Haj-Ayub, I travelled without incident of note, as far as the country of Damergu, and here my friend advised me to sell my Kano horse, telling me that it would surely die in the Great Desert beyond, and directed me to exchange it for a camel, which I did. For the space of two weeks we travelled through the Desert beyond Damergu, and the like of such country I never saw before. It filled my heart with terror.

Except at the wells and drinking-places, which were few and far between, there was not a sign of a tree or bush—nothing but sand, and hills made of sand. Although the land we crossed was so dry and parched and sandy along the line of the caravan, yet ever and anon, where the sky met the earth, I could see large lakes of water in the far, far distance, and groves of trees; but whenever I pointed these out to my companions, and asked why, when we were suffering from thirst, we should turn from these lakes, they would laugh and jeer at me for a know-nothing pagan, and tell me that these lakes were shams, and the work of the Jann who inhabit the Desert, and that, if anyone went in that direction, he would simply lose himself in the sand and die.

The farther we travelled the less I liked the Fezzani, Al-Haj-Ayub. He became rude and insolent to me, for each time I hinted at his handing over my slaves or paying me for the use of my camel he threatened to betray me to the leader of the caravan, and have me sent back to Zinder.

At length we arrived at Agades, and here I loudly demanded
my slaves and camel from Al-Haj-Ayub, and he replied, 'Assuredly, on the morrow, when we have rested, I will restore to
thee what is thine own, but speak not of this in the hearing of
the Tawarek that came with us, lest they find out thy secret and
inform the Sultan of Azben.' Accordingly, I waited with impa-
tience for the morrow, but on the morrow the Fezzani sent me
word that he was very sick with the fever, and could not trans-
act business, and, moreover, it would be better to wait till the
Tawarek guard was dispersed; but he asked me to meet him on
the next day in the market-place, and he would make over to
me my property. So on the morrow I met him, and he said, 'For
safety I have stored thy slaves and thy camel in another part of
the town: do thou come with me and I will show thee where
they are.' Then he led me through many streets to the house of
a Ghadamsi merchant, and when we entered he spoke to this
man in the language of Ghadames, which I did not then understand, and the Ghadamsi looked very hard at me, and said
to me in Hausa, 'All right, I will show thee where thy slaves
and camel are put, and thou shalt dwell with me till the starting
of the caravan for Ghadames.'

Then my Fezzani friend said to me, 'I have a matter of business to attend to, I will leave thee here,' and he departed. And
when he had gone the Ghadamsi directed me to follow him,
and led me into a dark chamber, and said, 'Look within that
inner apartment and thou shalt see thy four slaves.' And when
I turned from him to look, something struck me violently on
the head, and I swooned.

I know not how long I remained in that condition; but, when
I awoke, I felt very ill, and found my head covered with blood,
and my wrists and ankles tied. I was stripped naked, and my
dagger had been taken from me.

I began then to understand the trick that had been played

'The Mirage (These lakes were shams, and the work of the Jann).'

*'Then he led me through many streets to the house
of a Ghadamsi merchant.'*

on me; and, as I looked round, I found myself in the same dark chamber where the Ghadamsi had told me to look for my slaves. I staggered to my feet, and tried to find the door with my hands. But it was shut and bolted; and I struck it with my hands, and called loudly many times; but the exertion made me swoon again.

When I once more came to myself, I found the door open, and the Ghadamsi standing over me; and, when I looked at him, he spoke to me slowly and distinctly in Hausa, saying:

'It is time for thee now to know the truth. Thy friend the Fezzani has played thee a trick. Here are no slaves of thine, nor yet a camel; and I doubt much whether thou hast ever possessed any, for the Fezzani said thou wert a mad fellow that pestered him with thy tales, and he paid me to detain thee here until such time as he should have started well on his return to Ghadames. Now, hearken carefully to what I say. Whether or no thou hadst slaves is a matter of no interest to me. Thou art now *my* slave. If thou art disposed to work for me without noise or clamour, it is well. I will give thee food and clothing, and treat thee well. But if thou art going to make a rumpus and bother with thy talk of slaves and camels, it were better that I put an end to thee at once before thy strength comes back.'

And here he held above me my own dagger, and made a feint as it were to plunge it into my breast; but I, feebly staying him with my hand, begged for mercy, and told him that since I could not recover my property, and had nowhere to go for protection, I would remain with him, and serve him faithfully as his slave.

At these words he put the dagger back into its sheath, and lifted me up and led me into an outer court, where he bade me wash my wounded head in a tank of water, and, afterwards, he gave me a mess of porridge and an old shirt.

And in this sorry condition I abode with the Ghadamsi for a space of three months. And then he concluded his business in

Ghadames, and, having gathered together a large convoy of slaves, he made ready to return to his native town. So we set out with the next Ghadames caravan.

Whilst we journeyed through the country of Azben my life was bearable, for although I had to walk on foot, the marches were short, and there was plenty of water at each place we stopped at; but when we entered the Great Desert beyond our sufferings were terrible, for all we slaves had to walk on foot through the hot sand, and it was so far to go from well to well that many slaves died by the way; some would be able just to reach the drinking-place, and then would sink down and die before the water reached their lips. And if any slave was loth to start when the caravan was ready, he was either shot or left to die of hunger.

And in this way I nearly perished too, for when we had been journeying some thirty days a sickness of the bowels overtook me so that I could hardly drag myself along with the rest of the slaves, and I felt it was better to die quietly in the Desert than to endure this agony day after day. So when we had reached a certain well, where there was a broad wadi and many rocks, I managed to conceal myself among the boulders, and the rest of the caravan, hearing an alarm of the approach of some Tawarek robbers, hurried off, and no one searched for me.

In the shade of these rocks I fell asleep, and I must have slept a long time, perhaps a whole day and part of a night, for it was morning when I lay down, and the moon was high when I awoke, and instead of dying, as I expected, I felt somewhat re-covered, though my body was wet and cold with the heavy dew; but I cooled my parched tongue by licking the drops of moisture from my arms, and, in spite of my weakness, I managed to totter to the well which had been dug in the wadi and fetch up some water in a broken cooking-pot that lay near. I also found some dates and a piece of maize-bread, which some one in the cara-

'Many slaves . . . would be able just to reach the drinking place, and then would sink down and die before the water reached their lips.'

van had left behind in the hurry of departure.

Whilst I sat eating I had a great fright, for there was all at once a clamour amongst the rocks, and I thought it must either be the Tawarek coming, or the caravan returning. Then it seemed to me that it was not men that I saw leaping over the stones, but Janns or Ghuls of the Desert, and I was so scared with fright that the sweat poured out over me.

But when these creatures came nearer—I being too dazed to think of flight—I saw they were only baboons, of a kind not unlike those which were found in my own country. And they, too, were scared when they beheld me, and hesitated to come to the well to drink. But, finding I heeded them not, and seeing that I was unarmed, they gradually took courage and satisfied their thirst. And, when they had left, I again fell asleep, and did not awake till it was morning; and then I rubbed my eyes, and wondered whether I was under any more delusions, for I saw men standing and squatting round about me, and a number of camels tethered at a little distance, and these men had all of them face-veils, and I knew they were Tawarek; and when they saw me move and look on them, some of them started up and came towards me, and one said to me, in the Hausa language, 'We took thee for a dead man. How earnest thou here?'

Then I told them so much of my history as would serve my purpose; and, after consulting some time among themselves, one of them that had a spare camel that carried a little baggage mounted me thereon, and we rode away. After several days' travelling, during which the Tawarek treated me kindly and gave me a sufficiency of food, we entered a broad wadi, where there were many date-palms growing, and this, I was told, was on the outskirts of Ghat.

The Tawarek camped outside the town for a few days, and then took me into Ghat, and sold me in the slave-market to a Ghadamsi merchant, named Sidi Bu Khamsa. And here, in

'But when these creatures came nearer—I being too dazed to think
of flight—I saw they were only baboons, of a kind not unlike
those which were found in my own country.'

Ghat, I first saw the Turks. The Governor of the town and some soldiers who live in a fort are Turks, but the Tawarek are masters of the place. I do not think, although you are expert at travelling, that you would ever be able to reach Ghat, for the Tawarek will let no Christian come into the place; and, indeed, men that I met there would boast in my hearing of the number of Christians they had killed. Some they said were Fransawi,[81] who had come from the north, where the Fransawi ruled, and the Tawarek would tell how they had killed some with their spears, and had made others drink of poisoned wells, and for this the Turks never punished them, for they had not the power.

CHAPTER XVI.

I LED a quiet life in Ghat, and grew fat and strong, for there was plenty of food. My master, Sidi Bu Khamsa, was a mild man, and treated me kindly, seeing that I was a hard worker. He principally employed me in his gardens, which were in the wadi among the palm-groves, some distance from the town. Here I worked a noria,[82] which a camel turned round and round to bring up the water, and I tended the herbs and vegetables in the garden which the Ghadamsi was wont to sell in the Suk[83] at Ghat. I was happy here, and began to forget all my troubles, for my master, taking me into favour for the willingness with which I worked, gave me one of his slaves to wife, who was a native of Bornu. I lived in the plantations, and so little troubled me that I should have been content to have remained there all the rest of my days. But after about three years, Sidi Bu Khamsa died, and all his property was divided amongst his heirs. I, and my wife, and a lot of other slaves, were all to be sold in the market, because there was some dispute among the young men who claimed the property; therefore a day was appointed when the sale should take place.

Now some merchants had come from Murzuk for the purpose of trading, and when the auctioneer was leading us through the bazaars to show us to people who might wish to buy slaves, some of these Fezzani traders came forward to inspect us, and when one of them began to ask questions, I recognized the voice as a voice I had heard before, and, looking into the face of the man who had spoken, I saw it was none other than the Fezzani who had so well tricked me in the country of Azben, and nearly brought about my death. But I gave no sign of having recog-

nised him, thinking it better to bide my time and take my revenge surely. And he, looking into my face, knew me not, for I
had grown a beard and was otherwise much changed during the
time which had passed since we had last met. Moreover, the
Fezzani was suffering from the eye-sickness which was common
in Fezzan, and could not see clearly, so that when I was offered
him for sale he was obliged to touch my body with his hands to
ascertain that I was strong and well-made.

And the auctioneer, who was a kindly-hearted man, wished
that I should not be separated from my wife, so he asked of the
Fezzani a lower price if he should buy the two of us. And after
much haggling he consented, and I was handed over to him, together with my wife, for a sum of two hundred riyalat. Then he
took me away with him to the house in which he lodged, and
told me that he should return in a few days to Murzuk, and that
if I proved myself an honest and capable man he should put me
in charge of one of his plantations there. And to all that he said
I replied with sweet-sounding words; and though he asked me
many questions, and told me he had a fancy we had met before,
I said nothing, but concealed my thoughts from him. But to my
wife I told everything, and we arranged that we would wait for
a good opportunity to revenge ourselves on this man.

When he had got together all his merchandise and slaves,
and loaded his camels, we set out for Murzuk. Now the Fezzani
had taken a fancy to my wife, and resolved to make her his con-
cubine, and she conferring on this with me, I advised her what
she should do. In the gardens that we passed through outside
Ghat I plucked the berries from a certain tree,[84] and at the first
halting-place I gave these to my wife, telling her to bruise them
and put their juice into the Fezzani's drink, so that he might become stupefied.

This she was not able to do until several days were passed,
for the Fezzani sent not for her to come to him until we had ar-

rived at a great wadi between two high cliffs, where there was
much vegetation and abundance of fresh water, for it had been
raining in the mountains. Here Al-Haj-Ayub, who was ailing,
resolved to rest for a while, as in this place there were a few
abandoned huts, where some black people had at one time
lived, and in the middle of the first night after we arrived here
my wife came to where I was sleeping and said:

'I have done it. The Fezzani is now a dead man, or likely to
die. I ground up these berries with the coffee that he bade me
prepare for him, and now he is lying in his tent like a corpse.'

The other slaves were all sleeping, except two Fezzani servants, and these seemed to take little note of what was going
on near their master's tent. So I crept in with my wife, and
found Al-Haj-Ayub still living. He had vomited much of the
stuff my wife had given him, and when I crawled into the tent
he was making some effort to raise his head.

Fearing lest he should recover, I seized a big stone that kept
down one side of the tent, and with that smashed in the Fezzani's skull before he had time to cry out. And after this, afraid
for what I had done, I hastily took such small things as I could
lay my hands on—pistols and such like—and, beckoning to my
wife to follow me, we crawled out of the tent together and made
our way very quietly back to the place where I had been sleeping. And, being accustomed to this moving about of slaves at
night-time within the camp, the two Fezzani sentinels paid no
heed to our movements—perhaps even they were asleep. So I
passed round among the other slaves, such of them as were men,
and told them how and why I had killed the leader of the caravan. And we consulted together in whispers as to what we
should do. I asked them why we should always remain slaves to
these Fezzani and Ghadamsi people. Now that our master in
Ghat was dead, why should we not become freemen? And they
all agreed that these words were just.

Then I proposed that we should take the two Fezzani sentinels by surprise and kill them, and then divide amongst ourselves the plunder, and afterwards go our own ways. This being
agreed to, before the morning light had come, such of us as were
strong men armed ourselves, and, stealing up to the Fezzani sentinels through the rocks, we suddenly threw ourselves upon
them ere they were yet awake, and wrenched their guns away
from them. Then we stabbed them with knives and smashed in
their heads with stones, and they were soon put an end to. And
when the daylight came we divided the goods of the caravan,
not without some wrangling and dispute amongst ourselves; and
I, being the leader of the men, took Al-Haj-Ayub's camel, while
the camels of the two other Fezzani fell to the lot of other slaves.

CHAPTER XVII.

WHEN all these matters were settled we hardly knew what to do. Some advised that we should return to Ghat and tell a tale which should explain our case, and others counselled that we should continue on the road to Murzuk and enter the town separately. But as none knew the road, and we feared to lose ourselves in the Desert, I for one resolved to stop for the present where we were, inasmuch as the rains had left a great pool of water in the wadi and we had certain provisions of our master's to feed on; so, finding me of that opinion, the remainder of the people agreed to stay.

For the first few weeks everything went well. We patched up the abandoned huts with branches from the athal and talha trees of the wadi, and took up our abode in them, dividing the women slaves among such as were the stronger men; and we killed with stones and caught in snares the ducks and desert-fowls that came to the pool of water to drink; and we laid in wait for the great wadan,[85] the big animal with the mane something of the sheep-kind which you may find in some places in the Desert.

These wadan would come down in the night-time from the great cliffs that surrounded the wadi to browse on the sweet pasture which had sprung up round the pool. Our houses were away from the pool some little distance, half way up the cliff, and therefore the wadan were not disturbed by our presence.

So, in the darkness, we would creep down and lie among the rocks near the water, and, if the wind was in the right direction, and the wadan did not scent us, we would sometimes manage to kill them with our guns. But, after awhile, whether it was that these were scared away by our having killed some of their flock, or whether the camels were consuming the herbage, I do not know, but they ceased to come, and the ducks and other fowl, too, began to leave the wadi now that the drought was commencing and the pool drying up. And in this way we began to be short of food, and were forced to kill the camels one after the other, to eat their flesh. And when the scarcity of food was felt, before we had killed the camels, some of us were urgent that we should leave this wadi and proceed towards Murzuk. But it would seem that our master, the Fezzani, had chosen an unfrequented route, in order to avoid the bands of Ajhar Tawarek,[86] which are always ready to prey on small caravans in these countries, and that only he and his Fezzani companions knew in what direction the way should be taken towards Murzuk, for although we searched about in all directions we could find no issue from the wadi, which seemed like a track, and when we scaled the cliffs and looked round the horizon we could see nothing but sand hills and desert—no palm-trees or any sign of water, and I for one felt my heart fail me at the prospect of risking ourselves in the Desert with only three camels between us. So I was persistent in my resolve to stop, even though we should eat the camels one after the other, for, firstly, we had found a bag of seed-corn among the Fezzani's goods, and this we had planted in the moist ground near the pool; and, secondly, there was always the chance that another caravan of travellers might pass by to whom we could tell some plausible tale, and whom we might follow out of the wadi.

There were also date-palms growing near our house, but these being all females, and no one having fertilised them with the pollen of the male at blossoming time, they were without fruit, and all we could do with them was to cut them down one after the other and eat their hearts and young leaves. But as three or four months had passed, we began to be in sore straits—

'The great Wadan, the big animal with the mane, something of the sheep-kind . . . would come down in the night-time from the cliffs that surrounded the Wadi to . . . the pool.'

less from the want of food, though, than from the lack of water—for the great pool which had been formed in the middle of the wadi from the rains on the mountains began rapidly to dry up under the hot sun, and soon there was no more water left in it; and then for awhile we began digging holes in the sand to reach the water, which sank ever lower and lower. And as the water became harder to reach, and more and more precious, so bitter quarrels arose among us for its possession, and we fought for each water-hole, and, although I tried to keep order amongst the people, we were all mad with thirst and longing to drink, and in these fights one after the other was slain, and all the women except my wife died from want of water, for the men were greedy of what little water they brought up from the water-holes, and would give none to their wives, though with my wife I always shared what little I could get. At last matters got to such a strait that I said to those men that would listen to me:

'Rather than wait here till every drop of water is gone, let us start this night as soon as the sun is down, and it is cool, and walk over the Desert as fast as we can towards the west, so that we may perchance alight upon the first place we camped at before we reached this spot, where we may find water or meet travellers, and better were it even that the Tawarek should catch us, and hold us as slaves, than that we should die of thirst or kill one another.'

Most of them agreed that there was sense in these words, so we hastily threshed some of the corn which was ripe, and carrying a store of food and our guns, and such things as we could readily carry about our persons, we set out and walked as fast as we could, for the thirst that tormented us; but whether it was that in the darkness we could not find the traces of our former route, or whether the winds of the Desert had covered them over with sand, I do not know, but in the morning we could not tell what place we were in, or recognise any of our surroundings, and there was no trace of water anywhere. Our mouths were so parched that we could hardly speak.

When I dragged myself to the summit of one of the sand hills I could only recognise one feature in the country round me, and that was the great cliffs of the wadi, which we had left the evening before. And now we were in a sorry case; we knew not what to do. The heat of the day was so great that the sand seemed to burn us, and make our thirst ten times more dreadful, and some of the men were struck down by the way with thirst and the heat of the sun, and when we saw they were likely to die, we, who still had strength to move, threw ourselves on them and cut their throats, and then sucked greedily such blood as flowed from them.

In such a manner very few of us kept ourselves alive, and were able to walk a short distance, lying down every now and then to rest in the shade of such rocks as could protect us from the sun, and by nightfall we had arrived at the base of a small hill, where there were growing a few talha-trees. The dew that night was heavy, and in some places, where the rocks were smooth and free from sand, it lay almost as if rain had fallen, and here we obtained some relief by passing our tongues over the wet rock. Having moistened our mouths, we procured a little corn and swallowed it. When it was morning, we saw some Dum palms far away, growing in a little hollow. Our hearts were gladdened by this sight, because we knew it to be a sign that water should be there, and so we set out in that direction.

Now every day since we had left the wadi, where we had lived several months, when the day was at its hottest we would oft times see in the distance before us what appeared as great lakes of water, with palm-trees on their shores. This is some trick that the Jann of the Desert play on such men as are lost in those regions, for it is only a deception, as I have already told

'And she, too, after running for some distance, threw up her hands
and fell down in a heap.'

you. The further and further one walks after these lakes, the
more they recede, until, when the sun sinks, they vanish altogether.

The falseness of these seeming lakes and groves was known
to us, and we never diverted our steps to reach them; but on
this morning, when we set out to reach the Dum palms, my wife
was distraught in her head, and as the day grew hot and the
Jann's water began to show on the horizon, she would have it
that a great lake lay before us, and, indeed, thinking she was
back in her own country, she pointed to it, and called it the
Tshad, imagining it to be the great sea of Bornu. In vain I rea-
soned with her as well as my dry tongue would permit. She
would pay no heed to what I said, and although we were con-
vinced that we should find water at the Dum palms she would
hear nothing of this, but set off full pelt in the opposite direction, crying out that she could see her mother and the house
she used to live in. My strength was too little to enable me to
follow her and bring her back by force, and she, too, after running for some distance threw up her hands and fell down in a
heap. And then the others, my companions, crying out that
her death-hour was at hand, ran up and threw themselves on
her and cut her throat, and greedily sucked the blood. But I, in
spite of my thirst, had not the heart to join them, for even in
that time of madness I remembered that she was my own wife.
And after awhile a stupor came over me whilst I watched them,
and I slept.

When I awoke it was late afternoon, and there were none of
my companions round me. For some time I could not remember
what had happened, but when I gathered my thoughts together
I got up and made my way with such speed as I might to the
place where the Dum palms were growing, and here I found my
companions digging at a hole in the sand, near the base of one
of the palms, and the sand they were scooping out was wet, and

they were dashing it in their faces, and even cramming it into their mouths. I did the same to cool my tongue. Presently the water seemed to rise up between our hands, and at the bottom of the hole we had scooped there lay a small pool of water. With this we filled our mouths, washed out all the sand, loosened our tongues, and cooled our palates, and then each in turn stooped down to the hole and drank largely of the water. When our thirst was quenched, we ate of our store of corn and lay down to sleep.

The next morning we again drank our fill from the water-hole, and were loth to quit the place after all we had suffered. Two or three days went by like this until we were beginning to feel the pangs of hunger, and then we filled our gourds full of water and journeyed again westward, looking for some track we might follow.

Before we had gone half-a-day's journey we sighted a cara-van, and with great joy made up to them. We found them to be Fezzani merchants travelling to Murzuk, and to them we re-lated how our master's caravan had been attacked and dispersed by Tawarek, and that we were the sole survivors. Then the leader of the caravan took me as his slave, and distributed the rest of my companions among other big men of the caravan, telling us we should be fed and well treated if we behaved our-selves in a befitting manner.

After several days' journeying with no mishap we reached Murzuk, and here the leader of the caravan sold me to my pres-ent master Sidi Abd-al-Ghirha, who was a great man of the Senusiya brotherhood, and a Kaid under the Turks at Murzuk. Sidi Abd-al-Ghirha set me to work in his plantations, and being pleased at my behaviour, when he resolved to leave Fez-zan and settle in Tarabulus, he took me with him, for he is in favour with the Turks, and, as you know, a great man in this place. Is he not a Sherif—a descendant of the Prophet and

'For at this hour he is wont to leave the Mosque of the Olive Tree.'

learned in Mohammedan law? I have now been in Tarabulus perhaps six months.

This is the end of all I can relate to you of such things that have happened to me as are worthy of remembrance. I have talked too long to you to-day. Already it is time I saddled my master's *baghala* (she mule), and went to meet him, for at this hour he is wont to leave the Mosque of the Olive Tree. Now if I have pleased you by all the words I have spoken, show it to me in your generosity. What is this? Six—seven—eight riyalat! *Alhamdu-'lillah! Nasrani kulluhumkaram!*

THE END.

PRINTED BY
SPOTTISWOODE AND CO., NEW-STREET SQUARE
LONDON

Notes to the Text

(Bracketed notes beginning with "Johnston"
are H. H. Johnston's own footnotes reproduced from
the original 1889 edition of *The History of a Slave*.)

1. Mbudikum, a term referring to the grasslands and the Bamenda plateau north of Mt. Cameroon and the headwaters of the the Cross River. According to Warnier, slaves from the grassfields were known as Mburikum, Mbrikum, Mbudikum or Mbudikom, all variations of the same term. See Jean-Pierre Warnier, "The Transfer of Young People's Working Ethos from the Grassfields to the Atlantic Coast," *Social Anthropology* 14, 1 (2006), 93-98.
2. *Marghi*, the Hausa word for Tiv.
3. Fulfulde, the language; Ful/Peul, the people who, in Hausa, are re-ferred to as Fulani.
4. *Batta* = Bete ?
5. [Johnston: The Ful or 'Fula' people. *Pul-o* is the singular form (one Fulo man), *Ful-be* the plural. *Ful-de* or *Fulful-de*, the language. The Arabs call the Ful 'Fillani.'] Johnston's description is basically correct, except the Hausa term is *Fulani*, which was borrowed into Arabic.
6. Mayo Fombina, the river of the south. Fombina is an alternate name for the Emirate of Adamawa; see Sa'ad Abubakar, *The Lamibe of Fombina: A Political History of Adamawa, 1809-1901* (Zaria, 1979).
7. Kwara = Hausa for the Niger River.
8. Nufe is Nupe, but pronounced in Hausa, which does not have the phoneme "p."
9. I.e., Americans.
10. Tarabulus = Tunis.
11. [Johnston: Jargon, savage language.]
12. [Johnston: 'The Father of Strength,' the strong, lusty. A name some-times given by the Arabs to Negro slaves.]
13. Bahum = Bafum ?
14. I.e., amulets, small leather pouches containing sayings from the Qur'an that were thought to provide supernatural protection.

15. Bakuba = not identified.
16. Ghuls of desert.
17. Tibari [Johnston: 'Fula.'] = Tibati.
18. [Johnston: 'Prophet,' viz. Mohammed.]
19. The discussion of Epfumo suggests the *Ekpe* society; see Ute Röschen-thaler, *Purchasing Culture: The Dissemination of Associations in the Cross River Region of Cameroon and Nigeria* (Trenton, NJ: Africa World Press, 2011).
20. Asho-ntshoñ, the old 'Ñgañga,' not identified, but suggests *Ekpe.*
21. Cowrie shells, from the Maldive Islands and East African coast, were used as money in the Sokoto Caliphate and other parts of West Africa.
22. [Johnson: The Ful-be.]
23. Gashka = Gashaka, one of the sub-emirates in Adamawa under Yola.
24. Juku = Jukun.
25. Banyo = Banyo, one of the sub-emirates in Adamawa under Yola.
26. [Johnson: White men in Mbudikum.]
27. Dokaka and Jetem = not identified.
28. Mbum = Mbaum.
29. Yola = the capital of the emirate of Adamawa (Fombina).
30. Kotofo = Kotopo.
31. Ribago = possibly Rai-Buba, one of the sub-emirates in Adamawa under Yola.
32. Alantika Mountain near Ribago is not identified.
33. Ngaundere = one of the sub-emirates in Adamawa under Yola.
34. Yakuba = the emirate of Bauchi, often called by the name of the first emir, Yakubu.
35. Wusu on Benue = possibly intended to be Wase, just north of the Benue.
36. I.e., hippopotamus.
37. Basama near Benue = not identified.
38. Muri = one of the emirates in the Sokoto Caliphate.
39. Sokoto, the capital of the Muslim empire.
40. *dakakin* = *dakaki*, Hausa for shops.
41. Diwala = Duala.
42. *dukkin* = *daki*, Hausa for room or house.
43. Maria Theresa *thalers*, Spanish *douro*, and American silver dollars circulated alongside cowrie shells as the currency of the Central Sudan.
44. [Johnston: Christian.] *Nasara* = Christians, in Hausa.
45. [Johnston: Evil spirit.]
46. "Soso" = possibly Zazzau or Zaria, which was a separate emirate, not

part of Bauchi.

47. [Johnston: Fulful-de for ' Big Head.']

48. Wurno = the town established to the north of Sokoto as a frontier fortress.

49. Mohammed Sadiku was not the 'Sultan of Yakuba.' The reigning emir of Bauchi from 1883 until 1902 was Umaru, the grandson of Yakubu, after whom the emirate was sometimes called. Umaru succeeded Usman, his cousin, who reigned from 1877 to 1883.

50. Akpoto = not identified.

51. *Mai-doki* = 'owner of the horse.' The term for caravan leader in Hausa is *madugu*.

52. The description of Madugu Shekera suggests a comparison with the contemporary account of Madugu Mai Gashin Baki, who led caravans to southern Adamawa; see M. B. Duffill, ed., *The Biography of Madugu Mai Gashin Baki* (Los Angeles: Crossroads Press, 1984).

53. 'Two-bow prayer' refers to the Muslim prayer (*salat*); a full *raka'at* consists of two bowings (*ruku'u*) and four prostrations (*sujjud*).

54. Saria = Zaria, one of the emirates in the Sokoto Caliphate.

55. Tawarek = Tuareg.

56. *Mairini* = Hausa, *mai rini*.

57. *kurdi* = *kudi*, *kurdi*, Hausa for money.

58. Kano ward named Sherbale could be one of several wards.

59. The correct Hausa would be:

Mu masu rini ne.
Da fari [daga farko] muna rina rigar,
Bayan haka mu buga rigar,
In an jima sai mu tallata
ga mutum mai kyau [mutumin kwarai]

We are dyers.
First we dye the riga [male gown, long shirt],
Then we beat [indigo dye into] the riga,
And then we sell it
To a good [respectable] man

(I wish to thank Dr. Abubakar Babajo Sani for this translation.)

60. Galadima is a common Hausa political title.

61. [Johnson: Genii, spirits.]

62. 'Sarkin Yaki,' a common Hausa title, literally, 'Chief of War,' hence

Johnston's translation as captain of the guard.

63. Hausa = *sarki*, chief, emir.

64. Gujeba = Gujeba.

65. Kalam pagans = possibly the Kalam section of Kanembu.

66. Katagum = one of the border emirates between Kano and Borno.

67. Kola nuts were consumed for their caffeine; see Paul E. Lovejoy, *Caravans of Kola: The Hausa Kola Trade 1700-1900* (Zaria: Ahmadu Bello University Press, 1980).

68. Gubu is not identified, but there is a place between Katsina and Zinder near Kanche that is called Gobro.

69. Fititi is not identified, but there is a place in Damergu called Tikitit.

70. Zinder = Zinder, the western-most province of Borno, where Hausa was the common language.

71. 'Sarkin Bai' is a common Hausa title, 'Chief of the Slaves.'

72. [Johnston: 'The Laugher.'] 'Maidaria' = *mai dariya*, Hausa, the joker.

73. [Johnston: Aide-de-camp.]

74. Daura = Daura, one of the Hausa states divided by the jihad that established the Sokoto Caliphate.

75. [Johnston: 'Oh, great King, great King; King of the World!'] 'Sarkin Duniya,' Hausa, king of the world.

76. [Johnston: Slave-raids.]

77. 'Itatshe-n-mutua' = Hausa: *itacin mutua*, tree of death.

78. [Johnston: India.]

79. Engrizi = English ?

80. [Johnston: Aïr or Aïri, the name of the inhabitants of Azben.] The Aïr Massif is known as the region of Azben, of which Agadez was the most important city. The inhabitants of Aïr are referred to in Hausa as Azbenawa.

81. [Johnston: French.] Hausa, *faransi*.

82. [Johnston: Waterwheel.]

83. [Johnston: Market.]

84. [Johnston: Possibly the Datura or Thorn-apple.]

85. [Johnston: Ovis Tragelaphus.] wadan = ?

86. Ajhar Tawarek = Kel Ajjer Tuareg, centered on the oasis of Aghat (Ghat).

www.ingramcontent.com/pod-product-compliance
Lightning Source LLC
Chambersburg PA
CBHW030548030726
47495CB00004B/1181